Call Me Moose

Call Me Moose

Molly Cone

Illustrated by Bernice Lowenstein

Houghton Mifflin Company Boston 1978

Acknowledgments

My thanks to Joshua Dale for discussing in detail his favorite books and reading my first draft; to Peter Olson for "Ralph"; and special thanks to Michael S. Shuman for sharing his antler plans and moose history.

Library of Congress Cataloging in Publication Data

Cone, Molly.
  Call me Moose.

  SUMMARY: A shy, bookish young girl's decision to live up to her nickname exasperates and astonishes her family and friends.
  [1. Family life—Fiction. 2. Individuality—Fiction]
I. Lowenstein, Bernice.
II. Title.
PZ7.C7592Cal   [Fic]   78-1026
ISBN 0-395-26457-X

Contents

*To Mike S., whose moose call
inspired this tale.*

1

Pass the Lasagne

HARRIET'S THIN BLOND hair hung down over her eyebrows. Ordinarily her face looked like a peeled onion, and when she was excited, it glowed. It was glowing now.

Suddenly Martha was pleased that she had come to Harriet's house for dinner. She hadn't wanted to come, but now that she was here she was pleased.

Her mother and father had been pleased too. They were always pleased when she was invited any place. They always gave her an argument whenever she said she didn't want to go. "Put down that book and listen to me!" her mother was always yelling at her.

"Give Martha some more of that lasagne," Harriet's mother said. She was wearing blue jeans and holding the baby on her lap. She held on to him with one hand while she ate with the other. Every once in a while she stuffed a spoonful of food into the baby's mouth. Harriet's little sister, Frances, was sitting next to her.

"Maybe Martha doesn't like lasagne," Harriet said.

"Sure she likes lasagne." Harriet's father had red cheeks and all his hair. He picked up Martha's plate and plopped more noodles baked with tomato sauce and cheese onto the middle of it.

"Everybody likes lasagne," Harriet's mother said. She passed the plate back to Martha. "Eat. You don't have to be bashful."

"I'm not bashful," Martha said, feeling bashful. She wondered if she should tell them that at her house they never had lasagne. Her mother ordinarily never fixed anything with noodles or spaghetti. Her father didn't eat cheese or real butter. Her mother never wore jeans and her father always wore a necktie.

2

Harriet grinned at her from across the table. It didn't seem to bother Harriet to be all crowded up next to her sister's chair, or that Frances was wearing one of her T-shirts. Nothing particular seemed to belong to anybody special in Harriet's family. Harriet's mother often rode Harriet's bike, her sister sometimes slept in her bed, her father usually ate what Harriet left in her lunch box. Nobody in Harriet's family worried about calories, or cholesterol. They weren't always talking about football.

Harriet's sister was staring at Martha. She had long hair tied back with a purple hair ribbon. Martha tried not to notice an orange blob sliding down the front of Harriet's T-shirt, the one Frances was wearing. Martha held her elbows as close to her sides as she could and went on eating.

"Some more lasagne, Frances?" her father said.

Frances held up her plate. "It's revolting," she said happily.

"Ah shut up, Frances," said Harriet. Then she said to Martha, "She always says 'revolting.' She doesn't even know what it means."

"Yes I do." Frances took another bite. "Yum, yum. Revolting."

Martha hastily moved her glance from Frances' plate to her own. Frances had stirred some Jell-O into the lasagne. It was a mess. Revolting was the right word, Martha thought, and kept her eyes carefully on her own plate where everything was neatly arranged, nothing touching any other thing.

"What's really revolting to me," Harriet said, "is squash." She made a face. "Uggggh."

"Not to me," said Frances. "I hate squash."

"Look," said Harriet, "will you please shut up."

"Don't tell your sister to shut up," her mother said.

"Well, she's getting everything mixed up."

"I hate everything mixed up," said Martha.

"So do I," said Harriet.

4

Frances regarded them both suspiciously. Then she smiled at Martha. "You're revolting," she said sweetly. "But you're not." She glared at Harriet.

Harriet looked at Martha and Martha looked at Harriet and they almost fell off their chairs laughing.

Harriet's father started talking about adding a new room onto their house maybe, and Harriet's mother went two steps into the kitchen to get some more garlic bread, and Frances spilled some more blobs on Harriet's T-shirt. Martha went on eating. She was beginning to have a very good time.

"I saw your sister Audrey's name in the newspaper this morning," said Harriet's mother, sitting down again.

Martha looked up quickly. "What?"

"Your sister."

For an instant, Martha saw her sister Audrey. She was leaping into the air, her tennis racket up, driving a ball across the net.

She always saw Audrey that way whenever she thought of her, probably because of the picture hanging on the wall next to the door of the upstairs bathroom. Every time Martha walked in or out of the bathroom there was Audrey smashing a ball across the net.

"My, you must be proud of her!" said Harriet's mother.

"I guess so," said Martha.

"Well, she's made quite a name for herself in women's athletics," boomed Harriet's father.

"They even mentioned her favorite breakfast," said Harriet's mother.

"I guess they have to have stuff like that to fill up the paper," Martha said.

"I see your other sister's name in the newspaper all the time too," said Harriet's father. And he began telling everybody how Jeanne had been a swimming champion in high school, and had won the freestyle championship in college.

Martha didn't say anything. She didn't see what there was to say.

"Well it must be nice to grow up in a family like yours," Harriet's mother said.

"Yeah," said Martha.

6

Harriet's mother wiped the baby's face with a paper napkin. There were quite a few crumpled paper napkins piled next to her plate. Martha tried not to look at them.

"How does it feel to have athletic stars for sisters?" Harriet's father was dabbing butter on his garlic bread.

"It feels all right." Martha took a neat careful bite of her lasagne.

Harriet's mother put the baby down on the floor. "Well any day now I expect we'll be seeing your name in the newspapers," she said with a smile.

The food in Martha's mouth slid down suddenly and stuck in her throat. She put down her fork and took a gulp of water. She wondered how to tell them that she wasn't anything like her two older sisters.

She was clumsy. She must have been born that way because she couldn't remember a time when she had not been yelled at for having "two left feet," or "butter fingers," or "all thumbs." She was tall and gawky. She always had been taller than anyone her age she knew. She often stumbled when she ran, fumbled a ball when she tried to catch it, and always flopped every time she tried to dive.

She was just as awkward at anything else as she was at tennis and diving. She sometimes tripped over her feet just walking. There wasn't anything she could do about it, that's just the way she was.

"I'm no good at sports," she said loudly.

Harriet's mother and father stopped passing bowls of things around the table to look at her.

"I can't kick and I can't lob and I can't dribble."

Harriet's mother was still holding a bowl up in the air.

"The trouble with me is no coordination," Martha said in the same firm, positive way her mother always talked. And then she added, "I think."

Harriet's father leaned his elbows on the table. He started tearing off hunks of bread with his fingers and stuffing them into his mouth and chewing and looking at Martha.

8

Martha told them how she was always knocking into things in an absent-minded way. She always felt a little surprised when a ball she was supposed to catch slipped right through her fingers, or when her feet tangled up and she fell on her face. She never knew exactly how it happened. She even began to enjoy herself a little telling them what a goof ball she was.

"Well, sports aren't everything," said Harriet's mother, and she put a bowl of Cool Whip and dishes of strawberries on the table.

Martha gazed at the strawberries in the bowl as she ate, but what she saw was her parents sitting in front of their big color television set watching the Saturday game. They never missed a football game on television. They went to all the high-school games, and sometimes even to the playing field to watch the little kids playing soccer. Her mother had been a physical education teacher, and her father a Little League coach. Her mother could talk about hand-offs and blocks as easily as Harriet's mother talked about standing up and sitting down. And her father always read the sports page of the newspaper first.

Martha finished all her strawberries without tasting any. Maybe sports weren't everything to Harriet's parents — but, the trouble was, they were to hers.

2

The Reading Freak

MARTHA WALKED HOME from Harriet's, reading all the way. She held her book up in front of her face and walked up the block slowly, crossing the street with one eye still on the page, and turning in where she lived — at the oldest house on the block — without missing a line.

She went up the porch steps still reading. She kept reading until she opened the front door, tripped on the sill, and fell into the house. She was still reading when her book flew out of her hand.

"Martha? Is that you?" Her mother's voice came from the living room.

The faces of her two older sisters stared at her from picture frames on the wall. Jeanne posed in her tank suit, a winner's medal draped around her neck. Audrey looked down her nose, her tennis racket in her hands. Martha heard Audrey's voice clearly in her head. "Klutz!"

Slowly Martha picked herself up and closed the door.

She looked through the archway into the living room. More pictures were there — on the mantel, the piano, the table, the walls and standing on the wide bay window seat. Audrey running on the court, serving the ball, returning backhand, winning awards, and getting married. Jeanne diving and swimming and dripping, accepting trophies, and going to Europe. The living room was so crowded with pictures of her sisters that it took Martha a minute or two to perceive that her parents' friends, the Delsons, were in there too.

"That's Jeanne in high school with her state meet medal," her mother was saying as she sat on the sofa beside Mrs. Delson, turning the pages of the scrapbook. Her mother was smiling. She was smiling the

way she always smiled when she talked about Jeanne or Audrey.

Her mother was sitting with one knee crossed over the other, wagging her foot as she talked. Her mother never sat perfectly still. She was always wagging her foot.

"And that's the one the newspapers printed of Audrey when she won the state tennis championship."

Mrs. Delson's little ripples of praise were running in and out of the conversation like ants on a glob of jelly.

Her father was telling Mr. Delson how he used to coach Jeanne down at the park pool every Saturday, and how Audrey used to take her tennis racket to bed with her. Her father always spoke loudly and slowly as if he were saying something terribly important.

"Hi," Martha said, but no one heard her.

"Well," said Mrs. Delson as her mother closed the scrapbook. "Now that Jeanne and Audrey are all grown up, you still have Martha."

And then suddenly there was a big silence. As if there wasn't anything much anyone could think of to say about her.

"Hi," said Martha again.

Their heads all turned together. Mrs. Delson said "Hello Martha," and Mr. Delson winked at her and her mother automatically stopped smiling.

For some reason Martha suddenly thought about all the time her father spent trying to show her how to play basketball. Every Saturday morning he'd wait for her down on the driveway under the basketball hoop. He held the ball up in the tips of his fingers, like a waiter carrying a tray of pastries, and talked about shooting and dribbling. "You have to dribble with your fingertips instead of the palm of your hand. You have to keep control with your fingertips," he always said. Martha never had gotten the hang of it. She shifted her book from one hand to the other.

"What's that you've got there?" Mr. Delson always talked to her in an extra loud voice.

Martha looked down at her hands. She usually carried a book with her wherever

she went. She read while walking, or sitting on the bus, or eating lunch, or waiting for Harriet. She was reading right
through the library catalogue of Science
Fiction and Fantasy, and Myths and
Legends.

"A book," she said politely.

"A book, huh."

"What's the name of the book, honey?"
Whenever Mrs. Delson talked to her she
bent her head to one side and looked at
her as if she were trying to see into a mail
slot. Maybe that was because they were
exactly the same height.

Martha opened her mouth to answer,
but her mother said hurriedly, "Martha
had dinner at a friend's house tonight."
She said *a friend* as if she had lots of
friends.

"Yessirree" — that was a word Mr. Delson used a lot. "Certainly nice to have
friends."

Which reminded Martha's father of all
the friends Jeanne and Audrey used to
have. He talked as if they had to give out
numbers like in the bakery to keep all the

friends in line who wanted to sit next to them in the lunchroom, or stand next to either of them in the library, or walk home with them. Then her mother had to tell the Delsons how every birthday party was like a convention. She said she had to make oodles of cookies every day to serve to Jeanne and Audrey's oodles of friends. *Oodles* was one of her mother's favorite expressions. Harriet's mother didn't even know what oodles meant.

"*Finn Family Moomintroll,*" said Martha loudly and they all stopped talking.

"What?" said Mr. Delson.

"Speak up," said her father. "You can talk plainer than that."

"The name of the book," said Martha. "It's *Finn Family Moomintroll.*"

They all stared at her for an instant.

"By Tove Jansson."

"She reads a lot," her mother said quickly.

Audrey, framed on the piano, looked at her with a curling smile.

"A reading freak!" the smile said. "A real reading freak."

Martha went on through the empty dining room, past the china closet filled with tennis trophies, through the kitchen with its wall of ribbons and medals, up the back stairway, flanked by team photos and action shots, past the door to the bathroom and Audrey stuck in the air lobbing a ball, and into her room.

3

Two Peas in a Pod

ONLY ONE THING hung on the wall inside Martha's room — a sign. SLOW CROSSING CHILDREN. Usually whenever she looked at it, she felt like laughing.

Martha gazed into the dresser mirror. She saw the standard family nose, straight hair, which her mother always insisted needed shaping, fading freckles, a large mouth with small teeth and a long upper lip. She wasn't ever going to win any beauty prizes.

Reflected behind her were her library books and rock collection, matchbooks in an old fishbowl, and a neat stack of old jigsaw puzzles, no pieces missing, and Ralph — an eyeless black flop-legged

19

stuffed dog with a permanent grin sewn onto his face.

She glared at him.

"You'd better stop that grinning or I'll throw you in the trash can."

Ralph only grinned back.

The telephone rang and Martha went down the hallway again to answer it.

"My father thinks you're very funny," Harriet reported.

"He does?"

"Making up all those stories. He says you're a panic."

Martha looked up at the pictures marching along the upper hall walls. "He thinks I made them up?"

"He said —" Martha heard Harriet's sharp giggle — "he said we really are a pair. That's what he said. He said we're a *pair*."

"A pair of what?"

"My mother said — you and me — we're like two peas in a pod. She said that of all the friends I ever had you're the one most like me."

Martha felt a sharp stab in her chest. "Friends?" She felt herself wincing. "You have a lot of them?"

Harriet said quickly, "Well, I never had any like you."

Martha felt relieved.

"You and me — we're like soul brothers," said Harriet.

"Soul sisters, you mean," said Martha, liking the sound of it.

"It means we're buddies," Harriet said.

"I know — like Damon and Pythias," said Martha.

"Like who?"

"Well, there's this myth I read, about two friends. And they were called Damon and Pythias."

"Wild," said Harriet.

"Pythias was sentenced to death but he wanted to go to his sister's wedding before his execution. And the king said he could go if he guaranteed he'd be back. And his friend, Damon, stepped up and said, 'I'll be his guarantee.' Because they were buddies, you know. So the king said okay and Pythias went to the wedding and Damon took his place in prison. Three days went by. 'Time's up!' said the king, and he ordered that Damon be executed instead of Pythias."

"Wow!" said Harriet.

"And they led Damon out to the chopping block, and made him stick his head on the block and the executioner raised his ax. 'Where are you Pythias!?' Damon cried out. And just then Pythias came rushing in. 'Here I am!' he yelled. And the king was so impressed with the strength of this friendship that he let both of them go free."

"Hey, that's neat," said Harriet. "That's really neat."

"You can be Pythias and I'll be Damon," said Martha.

"Maybe we should be Laurel and Hardy," said Harriet. "That's easier to say — Laurel and Hardy."

"Laurel and Hardy! They were just a couple of comedians!"

"Well then how about Johnson and Johnson."

"The only Johnson and Johnson I ever heard of made Band-Aids," said Martha, feeling a little suspicious.

"Or Baskin and Robbins," said Harriet — going a little crazy. "Hey, let's be Baskin and Robbins. You know thirty-one flavors — chocolate, strawberry, vanilla mocha, chocolate fudge banana, peanut butter delight — " the voice at the other end dissolved into a chortle of hee hees.

Martha waited as patiently as she could.

"Hey," said Harriet finally. "You still there?"

"Lasagne," said Martha, making it sound like a magic word. "Two peas in a pod."

Harriet laughed. "You know what? You're a nut."

A nut. Martha hung up the telephone feeling pretty good. Harriet's parents liked her. They thought she was a "panic."

Martha went back into her room and closed the door. She focused her eyes on SLOW CROSSING CHILDREN. An odd feeling began to gather in her stomach.

Harriet's parents thought she had made everything up. They didn't know that she wasn't very good at making up things. They didn't know that everything she had told them about herself was the plain truth.

4

Sixty Minutes

IT WAS A GOOD dream. Martha saw her picture in the newspaper. She saw her mother smiling at her, and her father hanging her picture on the wall, and pasting a copy in the scrapbook. Martha woke up smiling.

Then she looked out the window and saw her father running up and down the driveway in his old Little League cap and warm-up jacket, with a basketball under his arm, and suddenly Martha couldn't remember what she was smiling about.

She took a deep breath and smelled the unpleasant odor of the marigolds bordering the driveway.

Every year her father planted giant

marigolds alongside the front driveway. He never planted anything else, only marigolds. Every spring, her father would get an argument from her mother about ordering dahlias or something she could cut and bring into the house. But he always ended up planting the same big, strong-smelling marigolds — maybe because they weren't good for cutting and bringing into the house. Her father liked seeing them along the driveway. He didn't change his mind very easily, thought Martha, or very often.

She rubbed at her nose, shut the window, and pulled on her clothes. He was waiting for her a little impatiently, and blew his whistle when he saw her.

"You ready?"

Martha shrugged. "I guess so."

"Now pay close attention. Shooting the ball into the basket is an art. An art, see?"

"An art," repeated Martha brightly.

Her father smiled. "That's right. Now in a way it's similar to swinging in golf. You can't have a good shot without

26

rhythm. And the rhythm is probably the most important part."

Martha nodded, only half listening. It was a nice day. She liked the smell of the daphne bush. Sweet. A little like the smell of cinnamon rolls coming out of the oven. Harriet's mother sometimes made cinnamon rolls. She could almost taste them.

"The most important part," her father was saying, "is that you have to keep your eye on the rim, feet square, and you can't rush it."

Martha stared at a plane rushing over-head.

"Martha!"

Martha's head jerked downward. It came down so fast that she felt a snap in her neck. She rubbed at it and focused her eyes on the ball in her father's hand.

"You've got to give sixty minutes of yourself in every game you play." Her fa-ther wasn't smiling anymore.

Martha hadn't ever thought of it that way.

"That's what Pop Warner used to say," her father said, just as if he knew Pop Warner personally. "Best coach in the world, he was."

Martha tried to think of herself as sixty minutes. She saw the face of a clock. The digital kind with numbers plunking up every minute. She wondered what time it was.

"That's what your sister Audrey did. Gave sixty minutes of herself. She always went all out on every game. Believe me, that's what made her a tennis star."

"I believe you," said Martha. She was beginning to feel a little hungry.

"Now your trouble, Martha — well you gave barely ten minutes of yourself. That's your trouble!"

The words rapped like knuckles against Martha's head, but inside she was already listening to the sound of the fire engine that could be heard coming up the street. Martha turned to watch the red truck go by.

Her father yelled at her.

Martha began to concentrate on the ball. She shot at the basket and missed.

"Practice," her father said stoutly. "All you've got to do is keep practicing.

"I'm not very good at it," she told her mother who had come out to watch.

"Well if you practiced more, you'd be better," said her mother.

Martha's father put a hand on her shoulder. He squeezed.

"I remember Jeanne, remember when she was going to high school. She wanted to quit the team. Well she took my advice and she didn't. And she went on to become a champ."

"You just haven't got your running legs yet," her father said.

"Or your throwing arm," said her mother.

"It takes practice," said her father. "At your age, Audrey used to practice all day every Saturday."

"I already promised Harriet I'd do something with her today," Martha said.

"Your sister used to take her tennis

racket up to bed with her," her mother said. She was sitting on a lawn chair, one leg crossed over her knee, and her foot wagging.

"I guess I'd better take a shower," said Martha.

The television in the living room was going loud when she came downstairs again.

Her mother and father were sitting in front of the television watching a varsity-alumni game.

Martha heard the snap of the ball and saw the line of players suddenly move. There wasn't even time for the quarterback to hand the football to someone else. No time for a pass.

"It's a blitz!" her father shouted. "You see that! It's a blitz!"

Her mother began to screech too. "Eat the ball!" she yelled.

Martha saw the player hug the ball to his chest just before the charging line piled on top of him.

Martha went on into the kitchen and helped herself to a bowl of raisin bran.

She ate it all, except the raisins. It took a lot of time and a certain amount of dexterity to avoid eating the raisins, but she did what her dad had advised. She put sixty minutes of herself into the effort, and finally succeeded. Somehow, it made her feel pleased. Just as pleased as if she had tossed the ball into the basket. But it wasn't the sort of thing her father would understand. As a matter of fact, she wasn't sure she understood it herself.

Martha sat there frowning at the little hill of raisins on the bottom of her bowl. The she got up, shook the bowl over the sink and turned on the garbage disposal. The demolishment took only a fraction of a second. She switched the disposal off and set the dish into the rack of the dishwasher.

Martha poured herself another glass of milk, ice cold. She liked it best ice cold. She set the glass on the table and sat down and opened her book.

5

You'll Love It

MARTHA TURNED THE page and heard her mother's voice as if it were coming from far away. She looked up. Her mother was standing right next to her. She must have been talking for some time, Martha decided, and quickly shut the book.

"Did you hear what I said?"

Martha picked up the glass of milk on the kitchen table and gulped. She made a face; the milk was warm. "Sure," she said.

Her father came into the kitchen with a couple of catalogues in his hands. Her father liked catalogues. Whenever he saw a free one advertised in the newspaper, he'd fill in the coupon and send away for it.

Half the garage was filled with old sports catalogues; her father never threw anything away. As far as Martha could see, the only thing her father had ever ordered from any catalogue was giant marigold seeds.

"What are you reading now?" Her father sounded pretty cheerful. He even sat down at the table across from Martha and smiled at her. But first he brushed at some invisible crumbs on the table top and squared off the place mat in front of him and spread out the catalogues.

"Well it's a Greek myth and it's about someone named Apollo who fell in love with a beautiful young girl named Daphne and wanted to marry her. But she was afraid of him. And he chased her, and she ran through the woods . . .

Her father picked up a catalogue and started to look at it. Martha began to talk a little faster.

"And she ran and ran. And she felt him following her and just when he was about to catch up with her she turned into a tree and . . ."

Her father didn't even notice when Martha stopped talking.

Martha finished her milk.

"A sleeping bag," her mother said.

"What?"

"You'll need a sleeping bag."

"What for?"

"For going to camp, of course."

"Camp? What camp?"

Her mother made a little sound of exasperation. "The same camp that Audrey and Jeanne went to, that's what camp. I told you all about it!"

Martha couldn't remember hearing anything about any camp and she said so.

"Not five minutes ago!" her mother said.

"I don't want to go to any camp."

"Don't be silly." Her mother picked up the empty glass and carried it over to the dishwasher. "You'll love it. Everybody does."

"I won't."

"I found Audrey's old duffel bag," her father said, looking up from his catalogue. He sounded terribly happy.

Martha's mother began to list off all the things she would need — "Flashlight, backpack, tennis shoes, pocketknife —"

"I don't want to go to camp," Martha said again.

They pretended they didn't hear her.

"You'll have lots of fun at camp," her father said loudly. "Jeanne was crazy about camp. Audrey never wanted to come home."

Martha stood there and tried not to see the flat faces of her sisters smirking down at her from the kitchen walls.

"I'm not going to any camp," she said.

Her mother smiled, a very careful smile. "You'll make a lot of new friends."

"I don't want any new friends."

"You *need* friends," her mother said. "Everybody needs friends," she said as if she were prescribing a spoonful of milk of magnesia for everyone in the world.

"I've got a friend."

"Everybody needs more than one friend," she said patiently.

"I don't."

Her mother began to look disapproving.

35

Which is something she did very well,
Martha thought. Better even than most of
her teachers. Her eyelids narrowed, and
her forehead wrinkled, and something
happened to her mouth. It looked a little
like an upside-down saucer.

"It's important to have friends," she
said. "Jeanne and Audrey always had lots
of friends."

"I don't like crowds," Martha said.

But her mother wasn't listening to anything Martha said. She was too busy talking herself. She pointed out that things
had gone far enough and something had
to be done and it turned out that it was
Martha she wanted to be doing whatever
it was that had to be done. And all
Martha had to do was stop being the way
she was and be more like her mother
wanted her to be.

Martha thought of her friendship pledge
to Harriet. *Soul brothers. Damon and
Pythias. Johnson and Johnson.*

"Lasagne," she said.

"What?" said her father.

"Two peas in a pod," said Martha.

And then her mother stopped wagging
her foot and started to yell at her.

6

Martha and Harriet

"I'm GOING TO CAMP," said Martha glumly.

Harriet was sitting on her stomach with her legs stretched out, painting a picture on her little sister's paint-by-number set.

It was a picture of a biplane, the kind used in World War I. It was all marked up into little spaces with a number in each space. All Harriet had to do was paint the little areas marked "one" with the color numbered "one." Then the "two" spaces with the color "two," and then the "threes" and so on through the "twelves." She was now coloring number five, which was blue.

"You mean for the rest of the whole summer?"

"Not for the whole summer," said Martha. "Only three weeks. It's a very special camp."

Harriet's nose was down in the blue paint now. "What's so special about it."

"My sister Audrey went to it."

"Oh."

"My sister Jeanne did too."

"But they're not you."

"Unfortunately, my parents act as if they are," said Martha.

"Unfortunately," said Harriet.

"The truth is, my sisters and I, we look sort of alike — on the outside." The thought of it was making Martha feel worse. "Too bad they can't see inside me."

"Once I saw a TV show," said Harriet, "about a bionic man who had x-ray eyes . . ."

"That's not exactly what I'm talking about."

Harriet raised her head. "You're stuck, huh?"

Martha gazed fondly at the enlarged smudge on the end of Harriet's nose. It was easy to like Harriet, no matter how sloppy she was.

"You're beginning to look like a rainbow ice-cream bar," she said.

Harriet grinned. She never got mad at anything anybody said.

"I went to a camp once." Harriet's nose was back down — a dime's edge away from the sheet she was painting.

"How was it?"

"Sort of like home."

Martha looked at her thoughtfully, then she glanced around at Harriet's room. Nothing was placed where it was supposed to be. It looked like the Seventh Street dump.

"And sort of like school too," Harriet said. She sat up. "What I mean is it's like having your mother and your gym teacher all rolled into one. Only they're called counselors." She went on painting some more.

Martha frowned at the twelve discs of color, set on the floor next to Harriet's nose.

"Everything was a little strange at first,"

Harriet said. "Even the food. But as soon as I got used to it, I liked it. Everybody did. Nobody wanted to go home."

"That's funny," said Martha. "That's what happened in this story I'm reading. After conquering Troy, Ulysses and his men were on the way home and they were all anxious to get there. But they came to the Island of the Lotus-eaters and they stopped to eat and visit. But what they didn't know was that as soon as they ate the food of the Lotus-eaters, it would make them lose all thoughts of home and make them want to stay there. And when Ulysses saw this happening, he had to drag his men off and tie them to the ships to get away."

Harriet stared at her a moment. "Bug juice," Harriet said. "Just to be on the safe side, watch out for the stuff called bug juice. They make you drink it at almost every meal."

She scratched her nose with a fingertip. Unfortunately, it was the finger of the same hand that held the paint brush, and quite a lot of paint landed on her forehead.

Martha looked at the painting of the two-winged plane. It looked as if it had collided with the sunset.

"You know what? I think you're finished.

"I am?"

Martha grinned. "As an artist, I mean."

Harriet sat up and regarded her work. Very slowly then, she placed her hand flat down on the wet surface of the painting. Then with a quick thrust she wiped it over Martha's face.

"Two peas in a pod!" she shouted.

"Lasagne!" screamed Martha. And she lunged at Harriet.

It was a pretty good tackle. She grabbed Harriet above the knees, and fell with her to the floor.

"Holy Moses!" yelled Martha's mother when she got home. "Who's been painting you!"

Martha stumbled up the stairs toward the bathroom. If she had made that same tackle out on the football field, she figured, her mother would have been proud of her.

7

The Moose in
the Window

"BLUE JEANS," her mother said when they got to the department store. "That's the first thing on the agenda."

Her mother always had an agenda, thought Martha. She made lists of things to do every day, and she hardly ever had to refer back to them.

"I don't need any blue jeans," Martha said not even looking up from the page she was reading.

"You have to have another pair of blue jeans," her mother said emphatically. "For camp you have to have a minimum of two pairs. It's the absolute minimum!"

Martha shrugged, and with her eyes still in her book she followed her mother down one aisle and up another. She leaned on a counter reading while her mother held a pair of stiff pants up to her waist. She turned when her mother said, "Turn," and held out her arm when her mother said, "Here, try this on."

They finally walked out of there with three pairs of jeans and a denim jacket to match and a couple of T-shirts. Her mother carried the package herself because as she said, Martha would undoubtedly lose it. Martha guessed she probably would and dutifully followed her mother out of that store and to the door of another.

"What are we going in here for?" she said when she saw the moose in the window.

"Sleeping bag," said her mother.

Martha trailed her mother around the mounds of sleeping bags for a while and then went outside to wait for her. She was just standing there facing a sign that said "Klineberg's Sporting Goods," reading her book when her eyes slid over and were caught by a moose in the window. For a moment Martha stared at the huge

44

antlers and great humped shoulders. Then she went back to reading her book, but for some reason she couldn't keep her eyes on the page.

She looked into the window again. The creature's large glass eyes stared out at her. Martha glanced over her shoulder then back at the moose. The eyes glinted.

The moose was standing on a plastic carpet of moss, near a swirl of sand that was supposed to be the edge of a stream or pond. Buried in the sand was a shallow dish with real water in it. Plastic water lilies floated on top. A stuffed squirrel was sitting on a big rock; a live fly buzzed around its head. It looked as if the moose had just stepped through a fringe of bushes and was surprised to be looking out onto a city street with buses going by and a girl gawking in.

Under the window spotlights, the wide spread antlers shone as if they had been freshly rubbed against the trunk of a tree. The moose had probably knocked down branches with them, thought Martha, when he reached into trees to nibble at twigs. He probably used them to scare off bears when he browsed through berry bushes.

He could have battled any animal with them if he wanted, Martha decided. But ordinarily a moose doesn't like to battle. He doesn't pay much attention to other animals — not even other moose — unless he's attacked or it's mating season.

Martha pressed her face against the window. The heavy shoulders of the moose were higher than the slim back end; he looked clumsy and awkward. Growing from behind its antlers were long mulish ears, and there was skin hanging under its lower jaw, just hanging, like a bell. Martha stared at the big bent nose of the head and at the long overhanging upper lip.

For a strange moment she felt those big antlers on her own head. She lifted her shoulders under the weight of them, carrying her head carefully erect. The glinting glass eyes of the moose stared into her own.

"Ugly looking beast," her mother said.

She had come out the store with a big package in her arms. She stood right behind Martha, staring over her head into the window.

Slowly Martha let her shoulders drop. Her mother handed her the package and started to search for her car keys in her handbag.

Martha suddenly wondered what it would feel like to be stuffed. She moved after her mother toward the car parked at the curb, and felt as if the moose's head turned to follow.

"I wonder what he's thinking," said Martha after they got into the car.

"Who?"

"The moose."

Her mother laughed at her. "He's stuffed," she said. "He can't think. Stuffed animals don't think." She rolled the package over onto the back seat. "You don't really think he's real, do you?"

She didn't give Martha time to answer.

"Of course," she said, staring musingly at Martha, "you used to think Ralph was real."

"Ralph is real," said Martha.

"Funny, funny," said her mother without smiling. She pulled out of the parking place, and blew the horn at a passing car. Her mother was a horn blower. Whenever there was a car ahead of her, stopped for a red light, she tooted the second the light turned green.

"The salesman wanted to sell me the Dacron-filled bag," her mother said. "But I said no, I didn't want a Dacron-filled. I said we got Jeanne a down bag, and we got Audrey a down bag, and that's what we want for you. I said it's a tradition in our family."

Martha opened to her place in her book.

Her mother glanced at her, and the smile that was on her face while she was talking about Audrey and Jeanne dropped away.

"Anyway, Ralph is real," Martha said, and she went on with her reading.

8

To Remember You By

MARTHA WALKED downstairs carrying Ralph and fell over the duffel bag set at the foot of the stairs.

"Martha?" Her mother's voice came from the kitchen.

She got up and went into the living room. Her sleeping bag was stretched out on the living room carpet. On the dining room table was her flashlight, pocketknife, a box of stationery, a canteen, and some other stuff. Piled on the kitchen counter next to the ironing board were a bath towel, a wash cloth, a pillow and case, four pairs of underpants, and six pairs of socks — and pajamas and jeans and shorts and T-shirts. She didn't bother to count. Her name on a tape was neatly ironed onto every piece.

"Don't touch anything!" her mother shouted at her.

"I'm not touching anything," she shouted back, and carried Ralph back into the hallway.

"Where are you going?" her mother asked coming through the kitchen door. "The bus will be here at exactly ten A.M. sharp," she added.

"I'm just going to say good-bye to Harriet."

Her mother stood on the porch watching her go down the street.

"Take it," Martha said pushing Ralph into Harriet's hands.

"What for?"

"So we can remember each other."

"You mean I can have it for keeps?"

"You're my friend, aren't you? I want you to have it."

"Hey, that's neat."

"Now give me something."

Harriet looked around her room. She was wearing her father's old tennis shoes and her mother's striped T-shirt. The toys in her closet belonged to her sister too, and so did her books. Harriet scratched her head.

"Anything," said Martha. "It doesn't make any difference. Just so it's yours."

"The only thing that's really mine is —" she plunged her head into the closet and pulled out a red shoe box.

"That's neat!" said Martha.

"There's nothing in it," said Harriet.

"That's okay."

Martha opened it. A ripe odor drifted out.

"Oops," said Harriet. "My dirty gym socks." She pulled them out and held her nose with her fingertips. "Pee-yoo! I guess I forgot about them."

Martha replaced the cover quickly.

"You don't want that."

"Sure I do. This is fine. Just what I meant." She stuck the box securely under her arm.

"Hey, I'll walk back to your house with you."

"Okay."

They walked slowly up the street. They didn't say anything for a few moments. Then Harriet said, "I'll take good care of Ralph."

"I know you will."

Harriet stopped at the street crossing. "Well, I guess I won't go any farther."

Martha stopped and turned around. "Yeah. Thanks for the box. Pandora's box," she said, remembering something she had read.

"No it's not," said Harriet. "It's my box."

"I mean a story I read about a girl called Pandora who was given a gift and it was a box only she wasn't supposed to open it."

"Not until her birthday, you mean."

"No," said Martha. "I mean never. But one day she opened it anyway and all these evils flew out, and she clapped the lid down in a hurry, but it was too late. There was only one thing left on the bottom."

Harriet stared at her. "What?"

"Hope."

Harriet scratched her nose. "Well there is positively nothing left in that box. Except maybe some smell."

"That's fine," said Martha. "It'll remind me of you." She tucked the box securely under her arm.

"As I always say," said Harriet, "a box in the hand is worth two in the bush." She grinned.

They walked across the street together.

A boy sitting in a window looked curiously out at them.

"As I always say," said Martha, "people in glass houses shouldn't have big ears."

A dog growled at them.

"What you've got to remember," said Harriet, "a barking dog blows no good."

"Yeah," said Martha, "and it's an ill wind that doesn't bite."

By that time they were already in front of Martha's house.

"Well, good-bye," Martha said.

"You don't have to write to me," said Harriet.

"I know," said Martha. She didn't really like to write letters.

"No news makes the heart grow fonder," said Harriet.

"Yeah," said Martha, and then she felt funny, almost as if she were going to cry.

"Anyway you have the box," said Harriet.

Martha blinked at it. "It's a nice box."

"You'd better not open it," said Harriet. "You know — it smells a little."

"It smells a lot," said Martha. "Anyway — I don't mind."

"Anyway," echoed Harriet, "it'll remind you of me."

They just stood there together.

"Ralph will miss you," said Harriet.

"He won't know the difference," said Martha.

"Sure he will," said Harriet.

"No, he won't. He's blind."

"That's so," said Harriet. "Well, so long friend."

"Soul brothers," Martha reminded her.

"Lasagne," said Harriet, grinning.

They said together: "Two peas in a pod."

"No matter how long we don't see each other, you'll still be my best friend," promised Martha.

"Hey! Watch out for the bug juice!" Harriet hollered as Martha went up the steps.

Martha laughed.

The front door was wide open. Martha walked in and looked at all her camp stuff piled ready in the hall. She didn't want to go to camp.

Her sisters stared coldly at her from the wall. Martha thought of the snake-haired sisters of the myths called Gorgons who turned men to stone with one look. She closed her eyes.

She saw herself running. She felt the wind sting her eyes and the branches grabbing at her flying hair. She took a deep breath.

"What are you doing now?" Her mother's voice snapped at her like the tip of a swinging branch.

Martha opened her eyes. "Nothing," she said. But she was standing as still as a slender bay tree, rooted to the ground, bending in the wind. And her name was Daphne.

Her mother said, "The bus will be here in a minute." And she went on talking. About how she had put Martha's name on the inside band of her underpants, and rolled her pillow inside her sleeping bag, and put her library books in the backpack, and how everything else she'd need was in the duffel bag, and she'd better go to the bathroom before the bus got there.

She didn't need to go to the bathroom.

"All ready?"

"Sure, I guess."

"Your toothbrush?"

She went upstairs to get her toothbrush

and came down with Harriet's box still carefully held under her arm.

"You have something in that box?"

"No, nothing."

"Well, what do you need it for then?"

She didn't bother to explain. How could she explain to her mother that the nothing in that box was more real to her than the everything in her duffel bag?

9

Cabin Six

HOLDING HER BOX close to her chest, and dragging the duffel bag, Martha followed the girls assigned to Cabin Six.

Camp Barker was just a big cleared space with some thin, tall trees around it and a still, flat lake beyond. A long, low building made of rough boards and old logs was the dining hall. And Cabin Six, like all the others, was stuck back among the trees.

Six cots were lined up inside. Six hooks on a long wall. Six boards made shelves in the space beside each bed. The place smelled funny to Martha, like moth balls and old pine needles.

"It smells the same," said one of the girls happily.

"Stop pushing," said another girl.

"We had five cots in here last year. How come six?"

"It's not the same cabin, dummy."

"What d'you mean, dummy?"

"Yeah, dummy."

"Owwwww."

"Okay guys," said the counselor, as she came in the door. She had a sunburned nose and a skinny voice. A whistle hung on a knotted string around her neck. There was a scab on her elbow and a clipboard in her hand. Across the front of her T-shirt was the name "Judy."

Judy looked at the clipboard, pointed to each girl and read out each name. "Lisa, Tami, Kim, Jennifer, Carol, and Martha." She smiled at them.

"Welcome to Cabin Six, Camp Barker," she said. "What's important to remember is that we're all here to have fun. And maybe we're going to get on each other's nerves once in a while, and forget. But if we remember that we're all one team, together, and look upon each other as teammates, and learn and play together, we'll grow together — and well — that's what's really important."

"Grow!" shrieked Jennifer. "My mother said if I gain one more pound she's going to send me to a Fat Farm next year instead of to camp."

"Fat Farm!" said Carol. "What's a Fat Farm?"

"It's where they grow fats, silly," said Lisa. "Haven't you ever heard of fats, before? They're delicious."

Jennifer giggled.

The girl named Tami raised her hand and waved it around wildly. "I went to a Trout Farm once," she said with great excitement. "And I caught some too. Three of them!"

Judy said firmly, "Why don't each of you choose a bed. Then unpack your stuff." And she took her clipboard and went out.

"I'll take this one," said Lisa. She had long skinny legs and long skinny arms and showed big white teeth when she grinned. She swung her stuff onto the nearest bed to the door and sat down.

"Well, I've got to sleep next to a window," said the girl named Carol. "I can't breathe if I don't sleep next to a window." She moved quickly to the only bed near the window.

"This is mine!" shrieked Tami as if it were better than any of the others.

Kim ducked her head and spoke into her cupped hands. "Blue Goose here, read me? Blue Goose! Just been sideswiped by Dirty Bird. I was headed for the breezy spot and she cut me off."

Lisa laughed. "Hey, Dirty Bird," she said to Tami. "You'd better let loose of that bed or you're going to get run over."

"I got here first!" screeched Tami.

"I can't find my duffel bag," said Jennifer. "Anybody got my duffel bag?"

"Hey you, Martha!" Lisa snapped her fingers. "What're you doing just standing there? Old Judy will string you up if you're not sitting down when she comes in."

"She's guarding her family jewels," hollered Carol.

Martha hastily dragged her stuff down

the aisle and plunked it all down on the only empty cot.

"Wall-to-wall and treetop tall," crooned Kim into her hand.

"Hey you, Blue Goose," said Tami. Pull the big switch. Or I'll pull it for you."

"She means shut up," said Lisa.

"I have to go to the bathroom," said Carol.

"Bathroom!" squeaked Tami. "There is no *bathroom!* At camp you don't pee in a bathroom, you have to pee in a latrine."

"You've got to follow that trail out back," said Lisa.

Carol went out and everybody else began unpacking their stuff.

"Wow," said Carol when she returned. "It's cold out there."

"When do we get to go to the bean store?" said Kim. "I'm hungry."

"What've you got in that box?" said Jennifer.

"Nothing."

"If it's cookies, we've got to eat them fast," said Jennifer. "It's against the rules to bring cookies."

"I didn't bring any cookies."

"Too bad." Jennifer grabbed one of Martha's books. She held it close to her face and read the title in a high, loud voice, *"Voyage of the Dawn Treader* by C. S. Lewis. Dawn treader? What's a dawn treader?"

"Well it's part of a whole series. See — first there was a book called *The Lion, the Witch and the Wardrobe* and it started with these four kids and they live in England and their father has a government job and they stay at this professor's house and it's a really big house and so they go into it and they find this room with nothing in it but this old wardrobe. So they open it and go in and they keep going. And when they end up they are in a land called Narnia —"

"Narnia!" said Carol. "I have a cousin named Narnia."

"My cousin's named Alexandria," said Tami.

"You have a cousin named Alexandria?" said Jennifer.

"Yeah, but everybody calls her Al."

"And the second in the series," Martha raised her voice to be heard, "is called *Prince Caspian* and —"

"Hey! Anybody have a brother called Caspian?" shouted Jennifer.

"Ah cool it, Jennifer," said Lisa, and threw a pillow at her. Only it didn't hit Jennifer, it hit Martha, and she pulled it off her head and hurled it back — but it whirled past Lisa and into the face of Judy who had just opened the door.

The counselor grunted. No one said anything.

Judy sent the pillow down carefully on the nearest bed. "Well," she said, "now that you are all acquainted . . ."

Martha carried her box with her when the lunch call sounded. She held it on her lap all the time she was eating. She kept it under her arm all during the welcome program, and carried it with her on the camp walk-around, and through the girls' baseball game that everybody had to watch afterward. She took it to dinner with her and then down to the firepit where everybody had to sit in a circle and sing.

Stretched out flat in her sleeping bag on the hard cot, Martha tried to remember what her room at home looked like. But the only thing she could bring to mind was the sign on her bedroom wall — SLOW CROSSING CHILDREN. Suddenly she couldn't remember why that had ever made her laugh.

Martha lay there rigidly. She watched the shadows moving past the windows. She listened to the branches scratching against the outside walls. She tried to remember how long it took after eating the Lotus-eaters' food for Ulysses' men to start forgetting. Staring up into the dark rafters she heard a skittering on the roof.

Martha listened to Carol snoring and Tami grinding her teeth and Kim bouncing up and down on her squeaking cot and rolling over and muttering. Even asleep, Kim sounded like a Citizens Band two-way radio.

When Jennifer got up to go out to the latrine, Martha reached for her box and held it close to her chest. She began to think of a story she had read about the giant named Argus who had a hundred eyes in his head, and never went to sleep with more than two at a time. Martha tried to go to sleep keeping one eye open.

She squinted down at the box under her chin, then poked at the lid and lifted it a little. The smell was still pretty powerful. She put the lid back on. But before she went to sleep, she reached out and pulled a shoelace out of one of her tennis shoes and bound the box up securely. Then she took the other shoelace and tied one end to the knot on the box and the other to her thumb.

She tested the knot, twisting it with her fingers again and again and again and finally set the box down beside her and closed both eyes. A Gordian knot, she thought with great satisfaction. It would take an Alexander the Great to figure out how to untie it.

"G'night, Harriet," she muttered to the box and went to sleep.

When she opened her eyes in the morning, the box was gone.

10

A Buddy

MARTHA SAT UP in bed. The cut end of the shoelace dangled from her thumb. "Hey, where's my box?"

"What box?" said Jennifer.

"It was right here last night. I left it right here."

"Hey you guys," said Jennifer. "Anybody see Martha's box?"

Lisa sat up. "Box? What box?"

"What'd it look like?" said Tami.

"Did you have a box?" asked Carol. "What kind of a box?"

Martha looked at the five faces. "Who took my box?"

"How big was it?"

The door opened and Judy came in. She was yawning. Every morning a different counselor had to go up to the flag pole and hit the big piece of pipe next to it with a stick. It made a loud clanging noise that was supposed to wake everybody up.

Judy looked at her feet a moment and then raised her head and looked all around.

"What's the matter, Martha?" she said.

"Well, I can't find something."

Judy's face grew a little wrinkled around the eyebrows. "You mean you lost something?"

"Well, I just can't find it."

Judy folded her hands behind her head, flexing the muscles of her fingers. "What can't you find, Martha?"

"My box."

"What was in it?"

"Nothing."

Judy stopped pulling her knuckles. "Well, no great loss then." She smiled at Martha.

Martha didn't smile back. "I want my box."

Judy frowned. "Hmmmmm," she said. "I see." But it was obvious that she didn't think there was anything to see. "Well, where was it when you last had it?"

"In my hands."

"Did you drop it?"

"No."

"Put it down someplace?"

"No."

"Well, Martha, if your hands were on it, I don't see —"

"I was asleep."

"Oh."

A sudden uncontrollable giggle leaked out from the other side of the room. Judy raised her head. She stopped yawning.

"ALL RIGHT!" she said loudly. "Give it to her."

Jennifer and Lisa sat up in their beds and looked uneasily at each other.

"Shake the tree and rake the leaves," murmured Kim into her cupped hand.

"Maybe she didn't lose her box at all," said Jennifer hurriedly. "Maybe it just dropped and rolled away, or fell under the bed —" She looked at Lisa. "Well, I wasn't the only —" she stopped.

"Ah, we were just having a little fun,"

said Lisa. She sat cross-legged on her bed, tossing her pocketknife up and down in the air.

Jennifer got out of bed and down on her hands and knees and began crawling under Lisa's cot.

"We didn't do anything to it," said Lisa, as Jennifer pulled out the box. "We didn't even open it."

"Here." Jennifer shoved the box at Martha. One shoelace still held it closed.

"Okay, you guys," said Judy. "Everybody up!"

They had to take their toothbrushes and towels and march all together up the path behind the cabin to the latrine. Martha straggled along behind.

"Hurry up," shouted Lisa to Martha trailing along behind them. "We've got to stay together!"

At breakfast they had to sit close together at long tables and eat scrambled dehydrated eggs and drink bug juice and sing wake up songs.

"Sing," mouthed Judy at her over the heads of the other girls. Martha opened her mouth and closed it again a couple of times. They had to sing a song about a prune-no-matter-how-old-it-grows-its-skin-is-always-wrinkled and she didn't feel much like singing.

After that, Judy led them back to Cabin Six where they had to make their beds. And then they had to get into their swimsuits and go down to the lake. Everybody had to say whether they were a beginner or an intermediate or advanced. The swim instructor was called Sara and she had a long bamboo pole and stood on the dock and directed in a loud voice.

"Everybody get ready to jump into the water," she shouted. "Choose a buddy. We don't go into the water around here without a buddy."

Martha stepped back. She had a buddy — Harriet. She didn't need another buddy.

"Get in there Martha," Sara said. "You're the only one who is still dry."

"I don't want to," said Martha.

"Sure you want to," she said. "Everybody wants to."

"Not me," said Martha.

Sara looked at her a moment, and then she blew her whistle and Judy came running up and they whispered to each other for a while. Then Judy rubbed the new skin on her nose and squinted at Martha.

"You don't have to be afraid," she said. "I'm right here."

"I'm not afraid," said Martha.

Judy smiled brightly. "Martha is going to sit this one out."

"Okay," Sara said.

She made everybody form a line in the water and go two by two and duck their heads and swim underwater.

She looked down at Martha sitting on the dock. "How about you, Martha? Changed your mind?"

Martha shook her head and sat and watched the swimmers.

Pretty soon it started to rain and everybody had to get out of the water. Then they had to change and go up to the arts and crafts building behind the dining hall and do things like make sand candles, or glue little bits of bark and stones and stuff to boards.

"You want to play dodge ball?" Jennifer said to her. "Cabin Six is going to stick together and play dodge ball."

Martha shook her head. She found a shelf of books and sat down on a bench and pulled some of the books out. She found one she hadn't read. It was called *Twenty Thousand Leagues Under the Sea* by Jules Verne. Martha started to read.

She took the book with her to the dining hall at lunch time. She ate through a bowl of soup and a sandwich holding her book in front of her and her box on her lap. She read right through all the screeching and yelling and singing. When she got to the last page and closed the book, everybody in the dining hall was leaving.

"Martha!" Judy called from the doorway.

Reluctantly, Martha put her book under her arm, picked up her box, and followed the others out of the room.

11

"I Don't Like Games"

"JUDY ASKED ME to check you over," said Belle, the camp nurse.

Martha shrugged. She sat down on the chair Belle pointed to, and looked around the camp infirmary. Through a half-open doorway, she saw a white iron bed with stiff white sheets piled on it. In the room where she was there were shelves with bottles on them and an examining table.

"You feel sick?" Belle put on a pair of glasses.

"I'm okay."

"Maybe homesick?"

Martha shook her head. She wasn't sure she knew what homesick was. She looked down at the box on her lap.

"You can put the box down on the table," Belle said.

Reluctantly, Martha placed it carefully on the edge nearest her.

The nurse put her fingers on Martha's chin, and twisted it around and peered down her throat with the aid of a little flashlight.

"What's in the box?" she asked while she was looking down there.

Martha pulled her chin away from the hand grasp. "Nothing."

The nurse looked into Martha's ears with another kind of light. "Well what are you going to put into it?"

"Nothing."

She let go of Martha's ears and snapped off the light.

"I was terrible in arithmetic," she said.

Martha stared at her.

"I used to hide all my test papers in an old shoe box." She nodded at Martha's box.

"I'm not hiding anything," said Martha.

The nurse looked out the window at the trash can out there and sort of smiled to herself. "I always used to be afraid that I'd fail. I was so afraid I'd fail that even when I knew the right answer, it didn't come out right. I was always afraid the teacher would find out how stupid I was . . ."

She gazed for a minute out over the can toward the lake.

Martha waited for her to go on. She waited for what seemed like a long time.

"Did she ever find out?" Martha finally asked.

Belle turned her head quickly to look at Martha, surprise on her face. Then suddenly she laughed.

She picked up the box and pushed it into Martha's hands "You're a wag," she said, grinning at her. "You know what I think? I think you're a real comedian."

Then she took her elbow and steered her to the door.

Martha walked back down toward her cabin. Judy was waiting for her in the doorway.

"How are you feeling?" said Judy.

"Okay."

"Fine," said Judy. "Then you just hop out there on the field and join the game. Cabin Six is playing against Cabin Eight."

"I don't like games," said Martha.

12

The Challenge

MARTHA STARED AT the coffee pot sitting on a warmer on the front part of the director's desk and waited for Mr. Hatcher to find her file in a paper carton stuffed with manila folders.

Judy had talked with her a long time. She had talked about being "a member of the team" and "pulling together" and being a good "team player." Martha had listened politely. For a while. Then she had stopped listening and picked up her book. That's when Judy had sent her to the director's office.

"I'll get to you in a moment," Mr. Hatcher said.

She didn't mind waiting. Through the window she could see the relay races going on. Martha shifted the box on her lap.

Mr. Hatcher glanced at her. "You can set that on the floor if you want."

"I can hold it all right," said Martha. "I don't mind holding it."

"What's in it?"

"Nothing."

Mr. Hatcher put a folder down on his desk and sat down too. "You carry it around all the time?"

"It's no trouble."

The director moved some stuff around on his desk. He scatched his chin and grimaced at the pile of junk in the corner. There was a big torn carton there over-flowing with footballs and bats and helmets. A Ping-Pong paddle had fallen over the side. And standing behind it in the corner was a broken canoc paddle.

"So you don't like games?" the director said suddenly.

"I don't mind watching them," said Martha quickly. "Sometimes I really like to watch them."

Mr. Hatcher rubbed his head. "Frankly,

your counselor has a lot of nice things to say about you, generally speaking, that is. But —" he stopped to regard Martha closely — "well, to tell you the truth, I've never heard of a camper who didn't want to take part in any of our sports."

She sat there, her feet resting on the rungs of the chair, her box on her lap. She folded her arms around the box so that she could feel its edges against her stomach.

"Well, you must like to play some games. What kind of game do you like best?"

Martha shrugged.

"Pin the tail on the donkey?" Mr. Hatcher grinned at her.

"I don't like parties," said Martha.

He gave a short laugh. "I never did like them much myself. All the beans always fell off my knife." He glanced at her. "That's a game. When I was a kid the one who could carry the most beans across the room on a knife won a prize."

Then Mr. Hatcher looked out the window at the kids running and screaming and hollering on the field, and back at

Martha sitting in front of him with the box on her lap.

"What do you like to do? For fun, that is."

Martha thought of herself and Harriet sitting on the porch railing having spitting contests. Or staring at each other to see who would break down and smile first. Or getting on the first bus that came along and seeing where it would go. Or sitting in front of the television trying to see who could hold her breath through the most number of commercials. Or sitting on the porch steps laughing. Harriet would laugh with a thin, high heeing, and she would yuk. Once they composed a whole symphony out of yuks and hees. Or just talking and doing nothing. That was fun. Sometimes that was about the most fun of all.

"Well?"

"Nothing," Martha answered.

The director leaned back in his chair. "Look here, Martha. There comes a time when a person has to prove something to himself, to move on to another area, meet

a new challenge and confront it success-
fully."

Martha sat there looking at the box on
her lap. She could hear herself say to Harriet, "Did you ever notice that this city has
a large population?" And she heard Harriet say, "Yeah, that's probably because a
lot of people are living in it." Once she
said, "The weatherman said we're due
for precipitation." And Harriet said, "I
say it looks like rain." Another time
Martha said, "All this fresh air increases
the appetite." And Harriet said, "It makes
you hungry too."

"Martha? Are you listening to me?"

"Sure," said Martha and she looked out
the window. The game was still going on.
"You said there comes a time when a person has to prove something to himself."

"Well?"

"I don't like sports," said Martha.

"I'm not talking about sports."

"Oh," said Martha and looked down at
the box on her lap. She thought that was
what she had been doing, hadn't she?
Proving something.

"I see what you mean," she said.

The director sat up straight. "Good! And there's one more thing — I understand that everybody in camp was at the soccer game this morning except you."

"Well, I watched for a while."

"And then?"

"Then I went down to the lake and sat in a rowboat."

The director frowned. "You know it's against the rules to get into a boat without a buddy."

Martha glanced down at her box. She didn't break any rules.

The director was looking puzzled.

"I didn't do anything," said Martha quickly. "I was just sitting in the boat reading."

"While everybody was at the soccer game, you were reading?" The director scratched his head hard, really scrubbed at it this time. "What were you reading?"

Martha started to think about what she'd been reading. It was a book she had found under the seat of the rowboat. She had never read anything like it before.

She started to laugh. "It's a real crazy book," she said, and had to laugh some more. "It's called *Sadie Shapiro's Knitting Book* by Robert Smith and it's this funny account of a seventy-two-year-old lady who jogs and knits and she starts up this business, see . . ."

The director sat there listening to Martha almost kill herself laughing, and then he closed up the folder on his desk and flipped it back into the carton.

"Look Martha, get outta here, will you?"

Martha stood up.

"And try not to make any more waves, will you? At least, try."

Martha walked down to the edge of the field with her box under her arm. She stood there and saw Lisa and Tami and Jennifer and Kim and Carol sitting together on a log watching the game. She went over and sat down on the log next to Jennifer.

"Hi! You want me to hold your box for you?" said Jennifer.

"No thanks," said Martha.

"What's the matter? You afraid I'll see

what's in it? What've you got in it anyway?"

Martha put her attention on the game.

Jennifer giggled. "I bet I know what's
in it. I bet I do."

"Brush your teeth and comb your hair,"
muttered Kim out of the side of her
mouth.

"What?" said Jennifer.

"She means watch out," said Lisa.

"Huh!" said Jennifer. She poked at
Martha. "You gonna tell me what's in it?
You are, aren't you?"

"Leave me alone," said Martha.

Jennifer moved closer. "Come on tell
me. Why don't you, huh? I won't tell
anybody. Honest I won't."

Martha sat there. She felt her back
stiffen, and the muscles in her arm growing tight.

"She's holding onto your mud flaps."
Kim warned Jennifer.

"Aw shut up, Kim," said Jennifer. And
she stuck her face close to Martha's. "I bet
I know what's in the box." She gave a
high, shrill giggle. "You got your boy-

friend's picture in there, that's what you've got. And his love letters."

Carol laughed.

Jennifer struck a pose. "Dear heart," she squeaked, clutching at her chest. "I love you, love you, love you!"

"I said leave me alone," said Martha. "You heard me!"

"You want me to prove it? Sure I'll prove it!" Jennifer made a sudden grab for the box.

Martha swung around, jerked her fist up and punched Jennifer in the arm.

"Ow-w-w-w!" said Jennifer. And then she rubbed her arm and shut her mouth and didn't say anything more.

That afternoon Martha wrote her first letter home.

Dear Mother and Dad:
I hate camp.
Sincerely,
Martha
P.S. I knew I would.

13

The Find

It RAINED for a couple of days. That didn't bother Martha any. While everyone was making candles, or sticking rocks and pieces of wood onto boards, or making faces out of potatoes, she sat on the floor in the corner reading.

She was almost sorry when the sun came out and the games started again.

Judy blew her whistle. "Okay you guys," she called. "We're going birding."

"Not me," said Martha and sat down.

"It's not a game," said Judy. "We take this" — she held up a pair of binoculars — "and this."

"What's that?" asked Carol.

"A bird identification chart."

"You mean we're going to *shoot* birds?"

"Not shoot them, sight them."

"Oh."

"Instead of guns we're going to use the binoculars. And each of you six will get a turn to use them and sight."

"Can I stay here?" asked Martha.

"No, you can't."

Martha retied her broken shoelaces and then trailed along behind the others with her box under her arm. She had visions of strolling around the lake keeping well behind the line so she could pretend they were nowhere about, but Judy led them directly to the slough that ran on the other side of the camp road. It was screened off from the camp area by a chain link fence and its banks were gone to weeds.

Judy made them sit down in the weeds in a circle so they could pass the binoculars from one to the other. They sat and they sat.

Martha stared around until her eyes hurt.

"Don't depend on your eyesight," Judy whispered. "The best way to see a bird is to hear it first. Just listen."

Martha listened. She didn't hear anything. She pulled her book from her
pocket, and, holding it down on her box
between her crossed legs, she began to
read.

It was a Greek myth about an inventor
named Daedalus who promised the King
of Crete he could design a dungeon for the
king's monster son, the Minotaur, who ate
men alive. And he designed a place un-
derground from which no man or monster
could escape. The king was pleased with
the clever labyrinth that Daedalus had
constructed. Whoever angered him was
thrown into this dungeon to feed his son.
And everything was fine for a while.
Then one day, somehow, someone got in
and killed the Minotaur, and the king was
so angry he cast Daedalus and his son,
Icarus, into this dungeon themselves . . .

"I hear something!" shouted Jennifer.

Martha looked up from her book.
Jennifer was pointing to a snag-top tree.

"An olive-sided flycatcher," said Judy.
She didn't even have to look at the chart.

"Pip-pip-pip," said Carol.

"That's not what I heard," said Jennifer. "I heard "Hic-three-beers.""

Everyone laughed. "Hic-three-beers," they kept saying. "Hic-three-beers."

"Quiet," Judy said suddenly.

They were quiet.

"Stop honking." Lisa made a poke at Carol.

"I'm not honking."

"Yes you are. I heard yank-yank-yank."

"Look!" Judy was pointing to a stand of green trees. Martha stared toward the place too but she didn't see anything.

"It's walking down the tree trunk," Lisa said in an excited whisper as she looked through the binoculars.

They all heard a nasal honk.

"A nuthatch," said Judy, and took the binoculars. "I think that's a red-breasted nuthatch."

Tami began to giggle. "Nuthatch," she said. "Old Lisa saw a nuthatch."

"Well it's more than you saw," said Lisa.

Then they sat and waited for a long time. Martha soon went on reading.

"Do we have to stay here much longer?" Jennifer was slapping at the bites on her ankles. "I'm getting hungry."

"There's a crow," shouted Carol, pointing to a black bird. It flew out of a tree and croaked at them.

"It's a raven," said Judy. "Crows caw, ravens croak."

"I once read a story about a raven," Martha said.

Judy waved her arm for silence.

Martha listened so hard that her ears began to ring. "I think I hear a meadowlark," she said quickly.

And they all sat there with their eyes sticking out but no one else heard it.

Then Kim sighted a jay. It was hollering and scolding at them, making a lot of noise. "Ratchet jaw," Kim shouted back at it. "Wall-to-wall and treetop tall!"

After that Tami saw a coot, and pretty soon Judy spotted a beaver dam and everybody wanted to look through the binoculars at the pile of stuff built across the stream.

"Beavers can see underwater with their

eyes closed," said Judy. "Their eyelids are transparent."

Martha closed her eyes for a moment and tried to read through her lids.

"Hey!" Jennifer poked at her. "Wake up!"

Then while they were all still passing the binoculars around and looking at the beaver dam, Martha finally saw something too. "What's that on the other side of the beaver dam?" she whispered.

"Over where?" Judy took the glasses.

"Near that old log that looks like a dead fish. It's blue," said Martha, feeling a little rush of excitement. Maybe it was something different. Something no one had ever seen around there before. She hoped it was something different.

Judy held the binoculars to her eyes for a long time. She held very still, studying it. Martha could just see herself telling Harriet about this rare bird she sighted. "And one day we went birding," she could hear herself telling Harriet.

"It's a very rare species," Judy said, and took the glasses from her eyes.

Martha held her breath.

"It's a genuine blue-topped, white-necked Clorox bottle."

"A Clorox bottle!"

"You mean all Martha found was an old Clorox bottle?" said Jennifer.

"That's all," said Judy, and looked at her wrist watch.

"A Clorox bottle," said Carol, and everybody laughed.

14

Wings

THEY SAT IN the middle of a meadow to eat their sandwiches. Martha ate and read her book.

She read how Daedalus collected all the feathers from birds devoured by the Minotaur. And how he laid them out overlapping in four separate rows, and fastened them together, some with melted wax and some with needle and thread. And then bent them and curved them into shape and made two pairs of wings, one for himself and one for Icarus. Then they took the wings and escaped from the labyrinth, and put on the wings and flew far from Crete.

"You want to come look at the beaver dam?" Judy was prodding at her.

Martha shook her head. When they all

had gone she closed her book, stood up, and looked around. She didn't see any feathers. If she had some, she decided, she could maybe try making some wings.

She raised her arms as if they were the wing bones of a bird, and gently flapped them up and down, trying to imagine how the feathers would feel as they gently rose and fell.

She began to walk in a circle, moving her arms experimentally so that the air caught the feathers on the wings. Then she started to run around the clearing. When she had gained some speed, she jumped and awkwardly flapped with her arms. She kept trying to jump higher and higher, flapping her arms faster and faster — until she stumbled and landed on the ground.

Martha got up again quickly. It took a long time, she remembered, for Icarus to get the knack of it. Martha started swooping faster and faster around the clearing. She could almost feel the air lift her high and she turned and soared, running faster and faster and getting hotter and hotter under the bright sun. She'd have to be careful, she reminded herself. What happened to Icarus might happen to her. He flew too close to the sun, and the waxed feathers melted, and he fell into the sea.

Martha rested a moment, her arms still outstretched. She felt the wind lifting the hairs on her neck and rustling through her wings. She saw herself landing on Harriet's porch and picking herself up and leaning on Harriet's doorbell.

"Hey! It's Martha!" She heard Harriet's excited voice. "Martha's back!"

"HEY MARTHA!" Martha opened her eyes. She saw Lisa and Jennifer and Carol and Kim and Tami staring at her from the edge of the clearing. Her arms fell like sticks to her sides.

They came in a bunch toward her.

"Hey! You trying to fly or something?" called Jennifer.

Martha said, "That's right. That's what I was doing. Flying."

Kim laughed.

Lisa poked at Jennifer. "You ask a dumb question; you get a dumb answer."

Carol opened her mouth and shouted, "Heehaw, heehaw, heehaw!"

The others laughed. All except Jennifer.

"As a matter of fact," said Martha, "I think it was a rather astute question."

"Astoot!" hollered Carol. "What's astoot!"

Judy came toward them blowing her whistle. "Okay you guys," she ordered. "Let's stop fooling around now. Get your stuff together."

Jennifer turned eagerly to Martha. "You want me to go get your box for you?"

"No thanks," said Martha and went to get it herself.

15

The Moose in the Thicket

"OKAY, EVERYBODY," shouted Judy. "Keep a sharp lookout. We're going back by the hikers' trail. Let's see what we can see." She led the way.

"Drop the hammer," muttered Kim.

Judy headed away from the stream and started up toward the forested hill. Martha stayed at the end of the line.

The trail crossed rivulets of water, and wound over mossy logs, and bare roots of trees. They walked through a stream, and crawled across slippery rocks.

"Time out," shouted Judy once. And by the time they had started up again, Martha had just caught up with them.

She stayed behind, sitting there for a while with her box on her lap. The voices of the others gradually drifted away on up the trail.

Insects darted, flying in and out among thick water lily plants. A squirrel jumped to the top of a nearby rock and sat there, still, when it spied her. Sunlight jabbed through the trees, spotlighting the carpet of moss and the blackish still pond. Martha blinked, and a moose was there staring at her through the trees. She saw the long-lipped face, the eyes glinting like the moose in the window of Klineberg's Sporting Goods store.

Jennifer came pounding back. "Here she is!" she began to shout over her shoulder. "She's still right here!"

"Anything the matter?" said Judy, appearing behind Jennifer.

Martha stood staring into the bushes.

"She saw something!" said Jennifer breathlessly.

"What did you see?"

"A moose," said Martha.

Jennifer cupped her hands to her mouth and shouted, "A moose! Hey you guys! Martha saw a moose!"

The others came jumping and running back. "Where is it? Where is it?"

Martha raised her arm and pointed into the dense green woods.

"A moose?" said Judy a little oddly.

"You mean you saw a moose, a real moose!" Carol was hopping up and down on the muddy path, trying to climb a moss-covered rock. She slipped and fell into the mud but nobody paid any attention.

"You're sure you saw a moose?" said Judy.

"Antlers," said Martha. And spread her arms.

Slowly Judy unwound the straps of the binoculars. She raised the glasses to her eyes, and stayed in one place, twisting her shoulders as she looked in three directions. "They don't usually come down this far," she said as she looked. "Not usually, that is."

"Ah, she didn't see any moose," said Lisa, and turned away.

"I did too," said Martha very loudly. "A big one."

"Hmmmmmm," said Judy, and put her binoculars away.

A thin giggle dribbled from one of the girls.

Judy gave a short blast on her whistle. "Pick up your feet," she barked. "You have fifteen minutes to get back to camp. Lisa you lead on, then Jennifer, then the rest of you."

Martha plodded on after them. She stepped over sharp rocks, by-passed mud holes, balanced herself carefully crossing a log that had fallen over an almost dry creek. And she stopped when they came to the camp road, and took a long deep breath.

"Hey Moose!" yelled Tami from the front of the line. "You see any more Clorox bottles?"

She pretended not to hear.

"Probably old Moose keeps her antlers

in her box," said Carol. "Is that what you keep in your box, Moose, antlers? Huh?"

After lunch Martha didn't even bother to write another letter home. She'd already said all there was to say.

16

The Box

FROM THEN ON her name was Moose. Everybody called her Moose. It didn't make any difference to Martha what anyone called her. With only one more week to go, she didn't bother to answer most of the time, anyway.

She read all Jennifer's comic books, and she used up a lot of time imagining conversations with Harriet. She thought about Ulysses and the Lotus-eaters, and she started to drink the bug juice served every day at meals because she didn't have to worry about that anymore. Nothing could make her not want to go home.

She even rather enjoyed the last evening at camp with everyone sitting around the bonfire making "some-mores" out of marshmallows and graham crackers and

Hershey bars, and singing the "wrinkled-prune" songs. She enjoyed it most of all because it was her last evening there. That's why she enjoyed it.

First thing the next morning, everybody had to pack their stuff and sweep under their beds. And after breakfast they had to take everything out to the field behind the dining hall where the buses were being loaded. It didn't take long for Martha to drag her stuff up there.

She waited for the buses to get ready to leave, sitting on a bench with her box beside her. She sat with her eyes closed, pretending that her lids were transparent. She saw right through them.

She saw Jennifer with her belly sticking out under her shrunken T-shirt and a buck-toothed smile on her face. She saw Lisa with her arm around Carol. And Tami bending close to Kim. She saw all the other campers milling around and heard them screeching. She saw the buses loading the sleeping bags and duffel bags and foot lockers. She even saw Harriet's onion face glowing, excited at seeing her

again. She heard the slam of the side
storage doors as the gear was piled in.

"Bus is leaving! Bus is leaving!"

Martha hurriedly got up. She left her
box behind her on the bench. She didn't
need it anymore. Harriet would be there
when she got home, waiting for her.

Martha climbed onto the bus. She
looked for an empty seat.

"Martha!" shrieked Carol from the back of the bus. "We're saving you a seat!"

Martha felt herself being pushed through to the long seat at the back of the bus where Carol, Tami, Kim, Lisa, and Jennifer sat bobbing up and down. They pulled her down between two of them, squeezing her in. Everybody was pushing and shoving and screaming and yelling.

"Hold it down!" Judy was shouting outside below their window.

Finally everybody was on and quieted down and the driver started the motor. The door closed.

Suddenly Jennifer screamed — "Stop the bus!"

Everybody turned. "What's the matter?"

Jennifer's face was pressed against the window. "Martha forgot her box!" she hollered.

"Stop the bus! Stop the bus!" All Martha's cabin mates began to yell.

The bus doors flapped open and Jennifer went hurtling down the aisle. She jumped off the bus, grabbed the box left on the bench, and jumped on again.

"Drop the hammer!" shouted Kim, and everybody cheered as Jennifer lurched up the aisle, holding the box high over her head.

"You almost forgot it!" she said breathlessly as she deposited it on Martha's lap.

Martha looked at the box. "Thanks," she said.

"That's okay," said Jennifer grandly.

Lisa leaned over and pounded Jennifer's back. "Fast thinking," she said.

They were all looking at her approvingly. Carol and Tami and Kim. She sat squeezed amongst them between Lisa and Jennifer. All together on the back seat. Cabin Six.

Martha sat there with the box on her lap and a strange feeling in her chest. She stared out the window. Judy was smiling and waving.

"Ten four!" shouted Kim at the bus driver. "Let's start the flip flop!"

The bus started up again and everybody

began to yell. Suddenly Martha heard herself yelling too.

"Aw-aw-aw-awoo . . . ooooargh!" she bellowed.

Everybody began to laugh. Heads turned around, campers popped out of their seats. "Hey! Who did that?" "Do it again!"

"That was Martha!" Jennifer shouted.

Martha grimaced. "Call me Moose," she said.

17

Where Are You, Pythias?

WHEN MARTHA WAS let off the bus at her corner, the faces of Lisa and Carol and Tami and Kim and Jennifer were pressed against the back window.

"Good-bye!" they were shouting at her. "See you next year!"

Jennifer pushed her head out an open window. She waved wildly. "So long, Moose!"

Martha dragged her stuff up along the walk, past her father's stinking giant marigolds, up the steps, opened the front door, and fell in.

The television was going loud. The faces of her sisters stared cheerfully down at her. Martha picked herself up and closed the door.

"I'm home!" she yelled.

Her mother's hair was cut a different way. It was a different color, more red.

"How was camp?" her mother asked, while she moved the duffel bag from where Martha had placed it to another spot six inches away.

Martha shrugged.

"Did you have a good time?" Her voice was louder. Martha suddenly remembered that her mother's voice always grew louder when Martha didn't say what her mother wanted her to say.

"It was okay."

"What do you mean *okay?*"

"I've got to call Harriet," she said.

She dialed the number, already hearing Harriet's voice at the other end. *"Come on over!"* Harriet would holler at her. Harriet always hollered when she talked over the telephone. Maybe because there was always so much noise at her house. *"COME ON OVER!"* Martha grinned in anticipation as she listened to the ring.

"Hello!" said Harriet's mother.

"May I speak to Harriet?" Martha switched the receiver from one ear to the other; she shifted from one foot to the other. *"Come on over!"*

"Harriet!" Martha heard Harriet's mother shout.

She heard the telephone being set down.

"Harriet, where are you?" The voice came to the telephone from a distance. Martha heard sounds of shuffling and laughter and a baby crying and then all the sounds faded away to silence.

Patiently Martha held the receiver ready, close to her ear. Her ear began to grow warm with the pressure. No one came to the telephone.

Pythias, where are you?

"Hey, who left the telephone off the hook?" Martha heard. Then the phone was picked up. "Hello! Hello! Anybody there?"

"I am," said Martha hurriedly.

"Who is this?"

"Martha."

"Martha who?" said Harriet's father.

Lasagne. Two peas in a pod. Remember me, the panic?

"Martha Miller," said Martha.

"Well, Harriet's around somewhere. I'll have her call you when I locate her," said Harriet's father.

The receiver in Martha's hand began to buzz loudly. Harriet's father had hung up.

Martha walked into her room and stood looking at the place Ralph had always sat. The telephone rang.

She dashed to answer it. "Hello!"

"When did you get back?" Harriet's voice was high and breathless, too, the way it got when she had been hollering and laughing and having a good time.

"Just now," said Martha.

"You mean it's been three weeks already?" said Harriet. "I mean, well it feels like you just left yesterday."

"Well, it was three weeks, all right," Martha started to say but some of the words got stuck in her throat. She had to swallow.

"Well, come on over," said Harriet. "Me and Barb are doing the craziest thing. We're practicing for a magic show."

Pythias, where are you?

"Barb?" Martha said aloud.

"You know Barb. Oh, I forgot. Of course you don't. She just moved into the neighborhood. She's a panic! Knows all these magic tricks. Come on over and we'll show you our special disappearing act!"

Martha felt this odd tightness begin to gather in her throat. As if her neck were stretched out on a block and an ax edge was slowly coming down toward her.

Martha cleared her throat. "Lasagne." The word came out hoarsely.

"What?"

"Lasagne," Martha said again.

"We had some last night," said Harriet. "Barb stayed for dinner. She did this magic trick, see, right at the table. Frances thought she was revolting. She . . ."

Martha winced. Her face screwed up with a sudden sharp pain, real. As real as if her head had rolled off onto the floor. She hung up.

18

Water Lilies

"OH!" SAID MARTHA'S mother. She was looking in through the bedroom door. "I thought you had gone over to play with your friend."

Martha sat there on her bed. She didn't even bother to answer.

Her mother stood in the doorway looking at her, frowning slightly.

"Why don't you go play with that new girl?" her mother suggested.

Martha opened her mouth wide and laughed. Her mother jumped. Her mother acted as if she had never heard Martha laugh before.

Her mother said loudly, "Your father will be home soon. You can tell him all about camp."

Then she just kept standing there and looking at Martha awhile longer. "Your hair needs shaping," she said finally. She sniffed sharply the way she did at any unexpected animal. "You could use a bath," she said, and moved on down the hallway telling Martha to use soap — lots of it.

Martha got off her bed and gazed at herself in the mirror. She squinched her eyes and stared at her long, uncut hair, the bent nose, dark eyes, large mouth, and long upper lip. She raised her hands, palms out, fingers spread wide, and placed them like antlers against her forehead.

Out of the corner of her eyes, she saw the faces in the hall gazing at her. Martha moved to the doorway quickly. She walked along the hallway, lifting each picture, and turned its face to the wall.

"She's up there talking," Martha heard her mother say when her father came home.

"Who's up there with her?"

"Nobody," her mother said.

Upstairs, Martha tramped up and down

her room waving her arms about and saying "Arrruuuuwwwa!" and "Aaaaaaar" and "Aaaaaargh." She didn't go down until her mother called her for dinner.

"How was camp?" her father said when they sat down to dinner.

"Don't start asking her questions now," her mother said. "She's probably starved. Here have some chicken." She passed the platter to Martha.

"No thank you," Martha said.

"You mean you're not hungry?"

Martha looked at the chicken. For some reason, she didn't feel much like eating chicken.

"Not unless you have some nice water lilies," she said. "I really wouldn't mind having some nice tender water lilies."

"Water lilies." Her mother's forehead had creased itself into regular furrows.

"Well, actually, the roots. They're the tasty part you know."

"Leave her alone," her father said amiably. "You know how they feed the kids at camp. She's probably stuffed."

Stuffed. The word caused Martha a peculiar pain. "Arrrrruuuuuwwwa," she said.

"What's the matter? You got something stuck in your throat?"

Martha shook her head. "That's my moose call," she said.

Her father put down his knife and fork. "Your what?"

"My moose call."

Her mother laughed. "It's a joke. It's just a joke," she said to Martha's father. She turned to Martha. "Now eat your dinner, Martha."

"Arrrruuuuuwwwwa," said Martha.

"You want some more milk?" her mother said in that quick bright voice she used when she wanted to pretend that everything was just hunky-dory. That's what her father said when he meant everything was okay. Hunky-dory.

"Arrrruuuuuwwwwa," said Martha.

"Now cut that out!" said her father.

"Arrrruuuuuwwwwa!"

"It's just a little joke," her mother said again. "Isn't it, Martha?"

120

Martha took a gulp of milk and swallowed it. "My name is Moose."

"What?" said her father, but not very clearly. His mouth was full of chicken.

"Arrrruuuuuwwwwa!" said Martha. "Call me Moose."

19

Magic

MARTHA CROSSED OVER to Harriet's block. Frances was sitting on the sidewalk in front of her house drawing something on one of Harriet's old school papers.

"Aw-aw-aw-aaarh!" Martha said.

Frances looked up, scratched her nose, and selected another crayon from her box. "I bet you don't know where Harriet is," she said.

"Who cares?" said Martha.

"Maybe she's in her bedroom reading comic books" — Frances smiled at her — "and maybe she isn't." She tore up one paper and started on another.

Martha watched her as she made a round circle with a blue crayon. Then she took a pink and followed the upper part of the circle halfway around, and enclosed it on each lower side. She colored it in, holding the crayon on its side. She made ears and eyes and two triangles sticking out like wings behind the pink hair for a hair bow. She made a triangle for a dress and four straight lines for legs and big squares sticking in the opposite directions for feet. Finally she put little boxes under the inside ends of the feet squares for heels.

Frances stood back then and regarded her work carefully. "What do you think?" she said.

Martha thought of Harriet and Barb reading comic books together.

"I think it's revolting," she said and began to walk away.

Frances hollered after her. "They're hiding in the garage! So no one will see them. They're making a new magic trick!"

"Awwwr — awwwr — awwwr — aaa-aaaaargh!" Martha didn't even look back.

She ducked behind a hedge, and, bending low, scrambled along, dodging behind bushes until she came to the back side of Harriet's house. Some old boxes were piled up against the wall behind the garage. The window was broken. Martha could hear Harriet and Barb talking and giggling. Martha put a knee up on a box and peered in at the edge of the window.

The inside of the garage didn't look much different, thought Martha, than the inside of Harriet's house.

Harriet's father always parked his car and his motorcycle in the driveway. He never used the garage. It was full of boxes and suitcases, and old tires, and broken furniture. In the middle of everything was a wobbly card table with a black cloth on it. At one side of it stood Harriet, with her onion face glistening. And on the other stood Barb wearing a magician's cape over her shoulders.

"Now watch me," Barb was saying. "You've got to keep your lips together, see. And talk from down in your throat. But you've got to keep your lips still. Like this — *Howareyoutoday?*" Barb said with

her mouth closed. "Now go ahead, try it."

Harriet pressed her lips together.

"Aw-aw-aaaarh!" grunted Martha, and quickly pulled her head out of sight.

Barb started to laugh. "You're a rotten ventriloquist," she said to Harriet. "You sound more like some animal."

"I do not!" screeched Harriet. "I mean, I didn't — "

"Okay, okay," said Barb. "Try it again."

Harriet composed her face.

"Aw-aw-awoo . . . oooargh!"

Harriet stood there with her mouth open and a surprised look on her face.

Barb laughed. She nearly went crazy laughing. She doubled up, and slapped her knee. "Do it again!" she kept saying. "It's a crazy sound, but maybe we can use it anyway."

"I didn't do it," said Harriet.

"Sure you did," said Barb. "I heard it."

"No I didn't," said Harriet.

"You did too!"

Martha grinned. She moved slowly

away from the garage window, kept under cover of bushes and hedges until she reached the street again.

At the corner, while waiting for the light to change, she practiced her moose call.

"Aw-aw-aw-awoo . . . ooooargh!" Her lips barely moved.

A man waiting for the light to change rolled down his window and looked cautiously around.

"Did you just hear something?" he called to Martha.

"Hear what?" said Martha.

"A howl. Sounded like a wild animal to me."

"Do you think it sounded like a moose?" said Martha.

"A moose?" The man glanced at the distant hill through his rear view mirror, then looked over his left shoulder. "Did you see it?"

"I didn't see anything," said Martha.

"Well, I heard it all right. I certainly heard something like it." He shut the window and drove off, shaking his head worriedly.

20

Martha the Moose

AT HOME, MARTHA stretched herself out on the side lawn under the rose bush. She smelled the scent of the roses hanging above her and she turned her cheek to press her mouth against the smooth green grass. She nibbled a little at the grass tips. The taste of green. She went on nibbling a moment.

A screaming jet streaked across the sky. From the open window of the house, the vacuum cleaner whined. Her mother had just bought a new vacuum cleaner. Her mother bought vacuum cleaners the way she did everything else, Martha reflected. She used all sixty minutes of herself to find out which was the best investment. She went to the library and studied the consumer research magazines, she went to see demonstrations, she talked to various salesmen and lots of other people. By the time she was finished, she knew about every vacuum cleaner on the market.

Martha's mother never did anything without doing it sixty minutes' worth. She didn't just dust books on a shelf. She took out every book and dusted behind it too. Martha sighed. It would have been a lot easier on her to have a mother like Harriet's. Martha frowned and spit out a piece of grass.

The purring of her father's car as it turned into the driveway made her roll over and crouch behind the bush.

She watched her father getting out of the car. He was wearing a white shirt and necktie and his coat flapped open over his stomach. Her father was getting fat.

"Aw-aw-aw-aaaarh!" Martha said in greeting.

He took one look in her direction and turned and walked rapidly into the house.

The vacuum cleaner sound stopped. "You want an aspirin?" Martha heard her mother say.

"Damn it!" hollered her father. "No!"

Martha spent the evening lying on her bed. The murmur of her parents' voices down there in the kitchen made a pleasant background, sort of like the wind in the trees, or water whipping against the banks of a river.

Her father had eaten breakfast and gone by the time Martha arose the next morning.

"Good morning!" her mother said as if she had just personally splashed tons of sunshine over the world.

"Aw-aw-aw-aaaarh," said Martha, and went into the kitchen.

Her mother followed her in and stood watching as Martha opened the refrigerator door and closed it again.

"There's a nice new box of raisin bran," her mother said in high glimmery tones.

"Aw-aw-aw-aaaarh," said Martha, and found a bowl and helped herself.

"What are you planning to do today?" her mother said sitting down across the table from Martha. She sat sideways on the chair, one leg wagging a little more rapidly than usual.

Martha took a large spoonful of cereal. "Aw-aw-aw-aaaarh," she said.

Her mother slapped a hand on the table top. The bowl of raisin bran jumped. "Now listen here Martha — " She stopped to take a deep breath.

"Moose," said Martha.

Her mother started again — "You just listen here —"

Martha stopped chomping. She opened her eyes wide, hunched herself over the bowl, and pressed her top teeth over her bottom lip, stretching her mouth wide.

"My Gawd!" her mother said, interrupting herself. "You're even beginning to *look* like one!"

"Aw-aw-aaaarh!" said Martha feeling pleased. It was what she had thought herself, practicing before her mirror earlier that morning.

Her mother sat there staring at Martha.

Martha finished her breakfast, neatly wiped her mouth with her hoof, and moved with an ungainly stride toward the door. It was funny, but she was even beginning to *feel* like a moose. She said aw-aw-aw-aaaarh a couple of times as she mounted the stairs, walking as if she were large and clumsy, and humping over slightly. On the top step, she shook herself, and stomped some extra stomps.

Her mother was standing there at the bottom. There was a puzzled expression on her mother's face. "You feel all right?" The words came a little anxiously.

"Aw-aw-awoo-ooooargh," said Martha, and lumbered down the hall to her room.

She studied herself carefully in the mirror. She hunched over and stomped up and down, turning her head sidewise to see the effect. Her mother was right. She really was beginning to look like a moose, she decided. All she needed was a pair of antlers.

21

Coat Hanger and Cardboard

"WHAT ARE YOU looking for?" her mother asked after Martha had rummaged around in the miscellaneous knife drawer for a few minutes.

"Aw-aw-aw-aaaaaarh," said Martha and plucked out the grapefruit knife.

Her mother stood there watching while Martha went out to the back porch, found the masking tape where it hung over the work bench, helped herself to a metal ruler, a pair of pliers, a half-finished can of red spray paint, and a discarded empty dress box which said Nordstrom's on it.

"What are you going to do with all that stuff?" her mother asked.

Martha pointed to her head. "Aw-aw-aaaarh," she said.

"You'd better not mess up anything in the bathroom," her mother shouted after her. "I just scrubbed in there."

Martha carried everything up to her room. She flattened the box top and laid it on her cleared desk. She already knew exactly how she was going to do it. The pattern was drawn and taped to her wall. Now she stopped to study it carefully before outlining an antler shape on the cardboard.

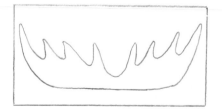

She cut around the lines with the grapefruit knife, sawing carefully through the rounded edges and up and down each point. Next she unbent a wire coat hanger, placed it on top of the antler shape in a

semicircle, and with the pliers cut off the pieces of the hanger that hung over the edge. Using masking tape, she affixed the wire to the antlers. The masking tape gave the antlers durability.

Then she spread newspaper on the floor and spray painted both sides.

While waiting for it to dry, Martha went downstairs and helped herself to an apple, chomping at it with loud chomps and pondering the eating habits of her fellow creatures.

"My Gawd! What a mess!" her mother said, coming into the kitchen.

Martha looked with surprise at the large number of crumbs and apple debris dropped around her. She didn't even remember when she had gotten up to help herself to the box of store-bought cookies on the shelf. She had, as a matter of fact, completely lost track of the number of apples she had eaten.

"Three!" her mother said, counting the cores. "You mean to say you ate three apples and a whole box of cookies right before lunch!"

Martha shrugged. It hardly seemed necessary to her to check her mother's reckoning. If her mother said it was three, she was willing to accept her estimate. Moose are normally pretty agreeable.

"Aw-aaaarrh," Martha grunted and went back upstairs.

The antlers were dry, with the kind of shine to them, Martha thought, equaled only by polishing against trunks of trees. Martha was pleased. She held her antlers up to her forehead. Then with masking tape, she attached them to the inside of a headband, one she had picked off her mother's dressing table. She rolled the tape around across the width of the antlers several times for strength, spray painted the new taped sections, and borrowed her mother's hair dryer to blow them dry.

The antlers felt good on her head. Martha lumbered carefully down the stairs, careful not to brush their tips against the wall.

Her father came out of his den, took one look at her, turned around and went back in. It occurred to Martha that her father had spent a lot of time by himself in his den since she had come home from camp.

22

Michael

MARTHA TROMPED slowly through the neighborhood with the antlers on her head. Every once in a while she stopped and gave her moose call.

A woman shaking a blanket over her porch railing heard her and dropped the blanket on the rose bushes. Two boys stopped, turned around, and grinned. A man walking with a cane, leaned on it and laughed.

"Aw-aw-aw-awoo . . . ooooargh!" Martha bellowed, feeling happy, and crossed over to another street.

A boy was sitting on the curb in front of a newly painted house reading. She had never seen him around there before. Empty cartons filled the driveway and there were no curtains on the front windows.

"Aw-aw-aw-aaaargh!" Martha said walking past him.

The boy looked up briefly, then down again at his book.

Martha stopped and turned around. She couldn't help staring.

He glanced up again at her. His face had an odd look as if it were made up of halves of two different faces. His eyes flicked over her antlers. One of them was blue and the other was not. "Lummox," he muttered.

"Moose," she said quickly.

For a moment his gaze settled on her face blankly. Then he shook his head. "I mean my book. If that's what you were staring at. It's about a lummox. Science fiction."

"*The Star Beast*," she said trying to keep from looking at his unmatched eyes. "By Robert Heinlein."

He regarded her speculatively. "Flat cat?"

Martha snapped her fingers. "*The Roll-*

ing Stones. Same author." She had read all the science fiction books by Robert Heinlein. They all had strange creatures in them.

The boy stuck his finger in his book to keep his place. "Have you ever read *A Wrinkle in Time?*" He went on quickly — "It's about these three children, and their father is a scientist . . ."

". . . and he vanishes," said Martha just as quickly, "and they're afraid he's no longer on the planet Earth so they search for him."

The boy with the odd eyes gave an abrupt shake of his head. She hardly noticed his eyes when he smiled.

Martha leaned against the fire hydrant and smiled back. *"Star Dog?"*

"By A. M. Lightner!" he said. "It's about this six-legged dog —"

"Moon of Three Rings?"

He answered quickly — "It's about this Krip from another planet who transfers to the body of a four-footed creature —"

Martha nodded so vigorously that her

antlers almost fell off. She put up her hands to steady her headpiece and wondered how she had ever thought his eyes looked queer.

"I love science fiction," he said.

"Do you like stories about impossible people?" she asked him.

"Not if they're anything like the ones I know and I know a lot of them." He grimaced.

"I mean really impossible," said Martha.

"Lilliputs," he said. "Minnipins, Moomintrolls, Wombles, Fundinelves, Borrowers, Hobbits —"

"I mean Gorgons," said Martha, "and Harpies, Cyclops, Furies, Satyrs, Sphinx —"

He said — "I thought a sphinx was an Egyptian stone statue."

"Well there's this Sphinx in a Greek myth. She's a monster with the head of a woman and the body of a lion and wings of an eagle, and she sat on a rock outside of the city of Thebes and asked every traveler who went by a riddle and if they didn't know the answer she killed them."

"What was the riddle?"

"What walks on four legs in the morning, two at noon, and three in the evening?"

He sat there thinking, staring at her antlers, not really seeing them. Then the front door of the house opened and someone called — "Michael!"

That was his name, thought Martha. Michael.

"I'm coming!" he yelled and scrambled to his feet.

She stood there looking down at him. The top of his head came to about her chin. Her antlers towered above him.

"I've got to go in now," he said. The lights in his eyes made two friendly bright points. He hugged his book to his chest and started toward his front door.

"Hey! Don't you want to know the answer?"

"I want to see if I can figure it out for

myself," he shouted back. "See you to-morrow!" And the screen door banged behind him.

Martha threw back her head and bellowed — "A-aw-aw-wooooooo   . . . ooooargh!" Then she galloped home.

23

Barb and Harriet

MARTHA PUSHED HER chair back from the table. "Aw-aw-aw-aaarh?" she said.

Her mother said, "Where are you going?"

"Awwwwrr-aaaarh," said Martha and went out the door.

Michael was sitting on his front porch reading. He stood up when he saw her. "The answer to the riddle is man," he said. "Because when he's a baby, he crawls on all fours, and when he's a boy he walks standing up, and when he's an old man he uses a cane."

She nodded and sat down on the steps.

"I looked it up in my big dictionary."

For a while they just sat there with their books on their laps reading. Michael was a very orderly reader. He never skipped anything. When he read a book, he started at the beginning and went straight through to the end. He didn't even skip the introduction.

Michael raised his head. "Do you think Pegasus would be a good name for a horse?"

"Sure," she said. "If it had wings."

He grinned.

"Argus would be a good name for a dog," said Martha thinking about the story of the giant, Argus, who had one hundred eyes.

"Well, Argus would be okay — if he was a watchdog." Michael went back to reading his book.

Martha grinned at him and returned to her own story. It was a Greek myth about a young man named Leander and a beautiful girl named Hero. And Hero had to live in a tower which stood at the edge of a four-mile wide strait called the Hellespont. And every time she put a light in her window, it was a signal for Leander to swim over.

Martha stopped reading to adjust her antlers. She had painted them with clear Varathane to make them shinier. All together she had given them seven coats and she knew they were perfect. Now she turned the shining prongs on her head and set them securely down against her ears, and went back to her book.

She read how one day there was a storm and Leander couldn't see the light but he tried to swim across anyway. But he didn't make it. And when Hero went down to the sea the next morning, she found him drowned, and she threw herself into the sea and drowned too.

Martha closed the book and thought about her parents not looking at television much anymore. She thought about them not talking about Jeanne and Audrey very much either. Her father kept saying he'd have to have his head examined if he ever sent Martha to camp again. He kept yelling at her mother — "I sent them a girl and they send me a moose! I'll sue them! You hear me, I'll sue!"

Martha smiled to herself. She sat there

thinking about her father and her mother and enjoying the silence — silence, that is, except for the sound of Michael turning the pages. She was really enjoying herself and would have gone on feeling that way if Harriet and Barb had not come flying by on their skate boards.

"Hi, Moose!" Barb hollered as they went by. But Harriet, busy trying to keep up with Barb, didn't even see Martha.

Martha gazed down the street, her thoughts reaching after them. *Two peas in a pod. Damon and Pythias. Johnson and Johnson.*

"Where are you, Harriet?"

"Or Cerberus —" Michael's voice interrupted. "I guess if I had a dog, I could name him Cerberus."

Martha turned her head slowly and looked at Michael sitting there with his finger marking his place in his book, and his two odd eyes squinting solemnly at her.

She made herself consider his words carefully, and when she answered, it was in a sensible, practical voice. "You could," she said, "if your dog had three heads."

And she was surprised when he laughed.

24

The Light in the Window

MARTHA SAT IN the dark in her bedroom and looked out at the moon for a while but she didn't feel like bellowing. She had left the light on in the bathroom, and the glow from the bathroom window shined down over the yard like a lantern in a tower.

She heard her mother coming up the steps and going down the hall. The light went out.

Martha took off her antlers and went to bed. But she didn't sleep well. She dreamed she was back in camp with Jennifer and Lisa and Carol and Tami and Kim. "Let's cut some z's," Kim kept saying in her dream. But all Jennifer wanted to do was go to the bean store and Carol was up near the ceiling flying around and saying "pee-ar, pee-ar, pee-ar." For some reason it was a terrible dream.

Martha woke up and looked at her antlers sitting on the desk. She went back to sleep and she dreamed Michael was swimming the Hellespont. Only her mother kept turning off the light in Martha's window and Michael kept losing his direction and he swam and swam and swam and pretty soon he couldn't swim anymore . . .

Martha woke up with this strange heavy feeling in her chest. She looked for Ralph's shape on the desk chair in the darkness. When she was a little kid and woke up in the middle of the night, she always looked for Ralph. But the only shape she saw was the rectangle of Harriet's box. And then she remembered that Ralph wasn't there anymore. She remembered that she had given Ralph to Harriet.

Martha sat up, got out of bed, and grabbed the box. She took off the lid and tore it in two. She ripped one end off and

then the other, and tore the remaining
piece into several pieces and pushed them
all down into her wastebasket. Then she
got back into bed and went back to sleep.

25

Ralph

THE DOOR BELL rang early the next morning. Martha set her antlers on her head
before going down to answer it.

"Hi!" Frances was standing there with
a blanket-wrapped bundle in her arms.

Martha glowered at her. "What do you
want?"

Frances smiled. One of her front teeth
was missing. "Can you come out and
play?"

"Arrrrruuuuuuwwwwwwa!" Martha
said and closed the door.

The doorbell rang again.

"Why don't you answer the doorbell?"
her mother hollered from the kitchen.

Her mother was a Sphinx, thought
Martha. Always asking her riddles.

Martha sighed and opened the door again.

"If you can't come out I can come in," Frances said, and marched in.

She stood in the hallway and looked curiously at the pictures on the wall.

"What shall we play?" she said.

"I'm not playing anything," Martha said flatly. She tried not to look at the smirking faces of her sisters.

"That's all right," said Frances. "Me and Michael will just sit and watch."

Martha's antlers almost fell off as her head jerked up. "Michael?"

"That's what I named him." Frances gave the pink bundle in her arms a hoist.

Martha felt the muscles in her chest tighten. "You named —"

Accommodatingly, Frances unwrapped the bundle. Ralph grimaced at Martha from Frances' arms. Old black beast Ralph with two odd buttons sewed on for eyes.

"Doesn't he look nice?" said Frances, and kissed him.

"Awwr-awwwr-awwwr-aaaaaaaargh!" roared Martha. The sound tore through the hallway and echoed up the stairs.

154

"For heaven's sake!" said Martha's mother, running in from the kitchen. "What's going on here?"

Frances said primly, "We're just playing."

"ARRRRRUUUUWWWAAGH!" Martha backed off, fell over the hall chair and started up the stairs. She fell halfway and crawled the rest of the way to the top.

"You'd better go home little girl," she heard her mother say sharply.

"I'm just going," Frances said. "I just stopped in to tell Martha that Michael doesn't love her anymore." She sent the last words hollering up the stairway.

Upstairs Martha bellowed madly. "AWWWRAAAAAAARGH!" She stumbled down the back stairs, and bolted out the kitchen door. She fell down the back porch steps and rolled into her father's marigold bed. When she got to her feet, some marigold heads clung to the points of her antlers, but she didn't care.

"AWWWR - AWWWR - AWWWWR - AAAAAAARGH!" She lumbered across the back yard, slashing angrily at bushes.

She ran across streets wildly, bellowing at any car that was in her way. She careened past Harriet's house.

"Hey Martha!" Harriet shouted at her from the garage.

"That's not Martha. That's a moose!" screamed Barb.

"Hey! Let's get her antlers!" shrieked Harriet.

Martha snorted, then whirled around. Screeching, Harriet and Barb chased after her.

Martha plunged across the street. Horns honked, people yelled, Martha reached the other side with Harriet and Barb close behind.

She crashed through a number of small hedges, swerved to one side or another when it seemed that one of the girls was close enough to grab her. She grazed her antlers against the branches of a cherry tree, threw her hands up to hold them, and, scattering broken twigs about, she tore down the street at a thundering gallop.

Martha didn't slow down until she came to the Crossroads Bridge, and a few seconds before her pursuers got there too, she flung herself down the pathway leading to the stream. She slid, sometimes on her feet and sometimes on her bottom, down the rocky embankment and stood there at the edge of the water taking great deep breaths.

"There she is! There she is!" Harriet's voice clattered down on her.

Martha felt her heart thudding. "Awwwwr-aaaaaaargh!" she yelled as they came tumbling down the embankment. She was cornered. The water was to her back and on each side the bank fell away.

Martha stood there, swinging her antlers menacingly, her feet set firmly on the pebbly ground. No one was going to take her antlers from her, she told herself. No one — least of all Harriet.

"Hand 'em over!" Harriet commanded.

"You heard her." Barb was grinning. "Hand 'em over."

Slowly Martha swung her antlers from side to side, hunching her shoulders and curling her fingers into fists.

Barb took a step toward her, Harriet too.

Martha eyed them, snorting. If she charged, she could knock them both down, maybe. She lowered her head.

Harriet stepped back. "Watch her," she warned Barb. "She's got a mean tackle."

Martha pawed the loose earth with her hoofs. For a few seconds there was no sound but the squealing of the cars going over the bridge above and the lapping of the water below. A cluster of little rocks rolled from under Martha's feet and plopped into the water behind her.

Across, on the other side, was a rim of trees, and beyond that, a parking lot. Martha inhaled slowly and with a quick sidewise movement, jumped feet first down the bank into the water. She kept her head up and her antlers high, and, swimming powerfully and well, she traversed the narrow stream and pulled herself up on the other side.

Shaking the water out of her face,

Martha stood peering across. Harriet and Barb still stood where she had left them.

"Awwwwr-awwwwr-aaaaaaaargh!" she roared defiantly. Then she resettled her drooping antlers, turned and loped off into the trees.

26

The Picture

MARTHA'S BLUE JEANS clung wetly to her legs, water dribbled from her hair down the sides of her nose. Her tennis shoes squished at every step. The antlers sagged around her ears.

"Aw-aw-aw-aaaarh," she called under Michael's window. There was no answer. She took off her antlers, raised her head and hollered — "Michael!"

The window opened and he looked out.

"It's me," said Martha. "Ask your mother if I can borrow your dryer."

Michael's mother lent her a towel, and Martha came out of the bathroom in Michael's too short bathrobe and dumped her clothes in the dryer in the kitchen. Michael was sitting at the table reading. She sat down across from him.

"Diana," he said, not lifting his eyes from the page. "There was this Greek goddess named Diana. And she was the beautiful twin sister of Apollo and was almost as tall as he was. And one day when she and her nymphs were in her favorite cave, bathing in a fountain, a hunter happened to wander in. And she turned him into a stag and the stag ran away. But his dogs didn't know that the stag was really their master and they chased him until they caught him and killed him."

Martha sat there with her elbows on the table and her chin resting on her hands, thinking about the story.

Michael flipped the pages. "The dogs' names were Melampus," he said, "and Pamphagus, Dorceus, Lelaps, Theron, Nape, and Tigris." Then he put his book down. "Hey, did you know? Your picture's in the newspapers."

"Me?"

"I guess it's you." He handed her the paper and turned back to his book.

It was her all right, thought Martha.

Someone must have snapped her picture when she was running down the street the other day. The funny thing was, it didn't look like her at all. It looked a little crazy. Martha put the paper down and went into the bathroom and took a look at herself in the mirror fastened to the inside of the door. It wasn't a very good mirror — the toilet and bathtub behind her were reflected wavily, as if through a veil of water.

She stood there in front of the mirror waiting for her clothes to dry. She saw herself standing there in Michael's bathrobe, her wet hair plastered down over her forehead, hanging over her eyes; her neck rising out of the robe, long and slender; her knees bare. The water in the pipes gurgled. Martha gazed into the silvery surface and for an instant what she saw through the veil was the wet walls of a cave.

Martha stared into the glass. In the mirror was Diana. A goddess — tall as Apollo and graceful as a deer. Who could, if she wanted, turn a hunter into a stag.

"Your clothes are dry!" Michael's mother hollered.

Martha shook herself a little, and went out and got her dry things and came back and dressed. She hung Michael's bathrobe neatly over the side of the tub.

"Tell your mother thank you," Martha said to Michael, her voice sweetly flowing.

Michael looked up. He nodded and followed her to the door and watched as she went down the steps and out to the sidewalk. She felt his eyes on the back of her head as she turned up the street.

"Hey! You forgot your antlers!"

Martha looked back at the soggy structure he was waving over his head. She hardly recognized it.

"I don't need them anymore." Her voice sang.

She went on. She passed Barb on the street and said, "Hi." And Barb looked at her a moment and said, "Hi," quickly and looked after her as if she couldn't remember who Martha was. Martha grinned.

Mr. and Mrs. Delson's car was parked in the driveway. Martha went up the steps to her house and opened the front door. She stepped carefully over the sill.

Voices were coming from the living room, her mother's loud and fast, her father interrupting whenever he felt like it.

"We have to call her *Moose!*" her mother was saying.

"She bellows," said her father. "Everytime she opens her mouth, the ceilings almost come down."

"The whole house shakes when she goes upstairs," her mother said. "She tromps."

"You wouldn't believe the mess she makes — apple cores everywhere, crumbs all over the floor, lettuce leaves under the sofa cushions."

"She takes her antlers up to bed with her." Her father's voice was grim.

Martha could hardly remember what they were talking about. It seemed like all that had happened a hundred years ago.

She walked past the faces on the wall and looked into the living room. They were all sitting around the coffee table looking at her picture in the paper. Her sisters' scrapbooks lay closed on the shelf.

Her mother wasn't wagging her foot or tapping her fingers. She was sitting on the edge of the sofa with her knees together and her feet set solidly on the floor. "Jeanne and Audrey never did anything like this!" her mother said.

"If you ask me, she's a whole new ball game," said Mr. Delson and cracked his knuckles as if he were winding up for a pitch.

Martha took a step, tripped over the edge of the carpet, and fell, sprawling, into the living room.

Everyone jumped.

Martha rose slowly. "Hi everybody," she said, her voice delicate as the green fronds of a fern.

Her mother said, "Martha?" as if she weren't exactly sure.

Martha peered at them through strands of hair falling over her eyes.

"Diana," she said happily. "Call me Diana."